The

Immaculate

Connection

D1211778

Also by Michelle Sawyer

They Say She Tastes Like Honey

The

Immaculate

Connection

Michelle Sawyer

alyson books
NEW YORK

© 2007 BY MICHELLE SAWYER
ALL RIGHTS RESERVED

MANUFACTURED IN THE UNITED STATES OF AMERICA

THIS TRADE PAPERBACK ORIGINAL IS PUBLISHED BY ALYSON BOOKS
245 WEST 17TH STREET, NEW YORK, NEW YORK 10011
DISTRIBUTION IN THE UNITED KINGDOM BY
TURNAROUND PUBLISHER SERVICES LTD.
UNIT 3, OLYMPIA TRADING ESTATE, COBURG ROAD
WOOD GREEN, LONDON N22 6TZ ENGLAND

FIRST EDITION: JULY 2007

07 08 09 10 11 a 10 9 8 7 6 5 4 3 2 1

ISBN: 1-59350-020-3
ISBN-13: 978-1-59350-020-7

LIBRARY OF CONGRESS CATALOGING-IN-PUBLICATION DATA ARE ON
FILE.

COVER DESIGN BY VICTOR MINGOVITS

For Big Clee, my old baby,
For Ava, my new baby,
And for Terri Fabris, editor and confidante,
for always going above and beyond.

About the Author

Michelle Sawyer was born and raised in Jackson, Michigan, "Home of the World's Largest Walled Prison" and "Birthplace of the Republican Party." For her first book, *They Say She Tastes Like Honey* (a 2003 Lambda Literary finalist), she toured the United States, speaking at bookstores, bars, Laundromats, libraries, and Vassar College. Currently at work on numerous projects, she resides in Michigan with her rottweiler, Ava, and a .357 she calls "Big Daddy," In her spare time, she reads, watches *Match Game* re-runs, and dreams of a world without the radical religious right. Visit her website at www.michellesawyer.com.

Chapter 1

"This might be the worst porn I've ever seen." I sighed. "And that's saying something." A meaty paw slapped a chocolate cake batter handprint onto the left cheek of a girl's ass, as displayed on our 52-inch flat-screen plasma. "This is why you should never eat anything someone makes at home and brings to the office potluck."

Faith, my charming wife, rolled her eyes and hit fast forward. The girls went at it at a frothy pace. I whistled the theme to *The Lone Ranger*.

"I take it this isn't doing the trick," she huffed. The "trick" being to get me, well, ready to rumble, so to speak. Upon hittin' fifty-two and having a four-year-old in the house, Auntie Men (as in "men-o-pause," the bad sister to Aunt Flo), or Auntie Myn, if you're a feminist, had arrived. Astroglide, trips to strip clubs, and now, bad porn…nothing could whip up the delicious goodness inside me. My pubes may as well have been tumbleweeds. I was as dry as the Mojave.

In spite of my plight, Faith deserved a good go. She wasn't even thirty. Why should she have to put her sex drive in park? I clapped my hands and hopped to my feet. Time to take one for the team. "Let's do it," I said, optimistic. "Let's give it a go."

Give it a go. Have it off. Fuck. Bugger. Punch the clown. I would boldly go where many a rubber dick had gone before. If one didn't have a sex drive, one could hitch a ride on the dildo express and strap on. All aboooooard!

"Yeah?" Faith's eyes widened. "You're serious?"

In a blink, she was buck naked between the sheets, and I was pep-talking myself in front of the bathroom mirror. "You can do this," I self-coached, fastening a buckle and feeling the leather back strap slide into the crack of my firm ass. *Gross.* "You're still hot, baby, still very Sigourney. You are not a pillow princess. You will fuck, and you will fuck heartily—even if you can't get off. Because that's the kind of woman you are." I wrapped my fingers around the mighty girth between my legs. "Just me and you against the world, tiger. We're goin' in."

Just then, my mobile phone rang, and I fished it out of my handbag. Constance.

Constance was my Alcoholics Anonymous sponsor. I'd gravitated to her as I cruised the throngs of haggard bores that fateful night last fall when I'd stood and uttered the words: "Hello, I'm Macy, and I'm an alcoholic." The room had been dimly lit and smoke-filled. The room had looked, well, like a bar, really. And Constance had been the only one wearing decent shoes.

"Macy?"

"Yes, Constance." I sighed, one hand on the phone, the other still on the pale, quivering schlong attached to me.

Constance had been a doctor before she bottomed out on Wild Turkey. The trigger of said belly smack into the booze was provided by a patient of hers. The patient, who was recovering from brain surgery, had walked out of the good doctor's newly furnished office on the west side to kill and dismember his wife of twenty-two years. He left his wife's head in a blue Tiffany box, complete with card and pristine white bow, on Constance's front steps. They found the rest of what remained of the wife mixed into the wet burritos at a taco stand on Fifth Avenue.

"God, I need a drink."

So do I.

As a sponsor, she was supposed to be helping *me*, thank you, but it didn't work that way. Constance called day and night, and there were times when her need for reassurance was intrusive. Obviously.

"No, you don't. You don't want a drink." I grabbed the tube of K-Y from the bathroom cabinet. "Say, is there any chance I can call you back?"

"Well, uh…"

"Look, I'll see you at the meeting Thursday. Don't wear your Hermès scarf or we'll look like the god-damned Doublemint twins, again." I lowered my voice. "And remember: one day at a time. It ain't just a sitcom, baby, it's our way of life, now."

Faith was waiting, squirming and giggling with excitement. I climbed into bed beneath the covers and felt her smooth skin against mine, the firmness of her breasts…

Mmmmmmmmmm…

Still, I felt guilty. Our four-year-old was asleep in the next room. What if he came strolling in during this little escapade? Did my insurance plan cover pediatric psychotherapy?

Ah, motherhood.

I had never wanted to like this baby. All my life I'd seen perfectly good women ruined by ten-pound babbling shit machines, and I didn't plan to join their saccharine ranks. Flashing pics of little Timmy with a snot bubble coming out of his nostril wasn't for me, thanks. But the kid grew on me. Not like a pustular growth, but like this silent, likable little stranger. He wasn't much for crying, seemed genuinely content to slobber on whatever was handy, and watched me with an openness and innocence I'd never witnessed before. William Behnke ("Banky") Delongchamp was as pure as Ivory soap, a boy without baggage. His soul seemed as snuggly and clean as his skin.

My first instinct was to feel sorry for the little guy for having entered such a world without so much as a Kevlar diaper to protect himself. Everything was his enemy: household cleaning supplies, hardwood floors, disposable razors, and plenty of other "innocent" stuff to choke on. While the world was sharp and scary for most of us, it seemed to have a particular grudge against babies.

At six months, Faith turned with him in her arms too quickly and bopped his head against a door jamb. He wailed for fifteen minutes, fifteen solid minutes, and I felt so helpless. Even if I strapped a helmet on the kid, it only guaranteed him safety in the arms of his clumsy mother. Outside of our walls, things were much more sinister. With each newscast, I felt convinced of his impending mortality. How could something so little, trusting, and ignorant survive when there were baby snatchers lurking around every corner?

Hence, the beefed-up alarm system in our apartment.

Hence, the new family gas guzzler: a Hummer.

Alas, life goes on, even with a kid to look out for. Curtain up, light the lights, it was time to service the wife.

I guided the faux extension of myself into her gently. So much for foreplay.

Faith moaned. "Oh, God...yes..."

"You're so beautiful," I whispered, and she was. Chin-length Aniston shag hair, crooked smile, big brown eyes, and Cherokee skin. She was also victim to my newfound Madonna/whore complex. After birthing Banky, the thought of her wanting sex almost pissed me off. She was a mother, goddammit. Mothers didn't need to be wildly fucked, or did they?

"Oh, baby, fuck me..."

Making love I could almost do. Fucking was a different story. Still, I had to muddle through this, somehow.

"My sweetheart." I let my lips come down to touch hers, my hips rocking slowly. My spine popped, and I was reminded that she was twenty-plus years my junior and considerably more flexible. Still, I trudged onward. I smiled. She smiled back. My sweet, beautiful wife. How could I resist such a perfect creature?

And then she said it.

"Oh, fuck me! Fuck me hard, daddy..."

WHAT?!

It brought to mind her merge with Marcus. Marcus, the good-old-boy back home in the sticks. Marcus, the Marlboro Man, the biological father of the son who carried my name. Marcus, who had a real dick, not this stunt dick I was wearing. I clenched my jaw. "I'm not your daddy."

Faith opened her eyes, no longer in the throes of, well, whatever fantasy she'd been in, and sat up. "I was only…"

I pushed her back, throwing her legs up over my shoulders and pressing in deeper. I could play this game, sister. It wasn't too strenuous if I kept my mind on other things.

Is it true that dogs are colorblind?

"Macy!"

Does this harness make me look fat?

I slammed my hips against her, slammed into her faster, harder, deeper…all the deep-dicking clichés applied. Faith had always discreetly referred to her privates as her "china" (her childhood mispronunciation of vagina), and I was about to shatter service for six—salad plates and all.

Did Brigitte Nielsen really fuck Flavor Flav on The Surreal Life?

"Macy! Oh! Macy! Oh!" A rhythmic chant, cheering me on.

Break that china! Break that china!

"Faster! Oh, God!"

Me, the human oil rig. My side ached. My back cramped.

I panted. I cursed. I conquered.

I conked out.

"Uh…Macy?"

Looking back, I fondly recall Faith's raven hair swung provocatively over one shoulder, her body a curvaceous silhouette to my dimming vision, her cute little finger dialing 911...

"Mrs. Delongchamp? Can you hear me?" A big boy in blue, with a name tag that read "Anthony Miller, EMT" leaned over me. Suddenly, I was in the back of an ambulance in the midst of a full-blown asthma attack, gasping, flailing, and wearing only a strap-on.

My mobile rang. Anthony flipped it open and held it to my ear.

"You never called me back. Are you angry with me? I really need your support."

Constance.

I grasped Anthony by the epaulet. "Save me," I croaked.

"Well, I'm not a doctor." He smiled. "But I'd say you're going to pull through just fine, Mrs. Delongchamp."

Chapter 2

When I was a child, our neighborhood had been bordered by more woods than farmland. Occasionally, I found it refreshing to jog through the trees that leaned toward the river, either to ice skate or to meet a stray girlfriend from a neighboring school district. One such girlfriend was dubbed "Rainbow Banana" by classmates, as she dyed her hair multiple colors and was known to proudly display her fellation abilities with a banana. Rainbow Banana would meet me under the bridge to kiss quite tenderly, but she was tough. Once Roger Horsford yanked her tube top down, and she chased him six blocks with a pocketknife until he tripped and started crying for mercy.

Anyway, it was coming back from a Rainbow Banana bridge excursion that I saw something moving far ahead on my path through the woods. I was startled, initially thinking it was a person writhing on the ground. Closer inspection proved the wriggling mass to be a beagle caught in a trap.

She'd been there long enough to shit on herself and was too weak to raise her head for more than a few seconds. My head spun with panic. I felt sick. The teeth of the trap bit hard into the flesh of her leg. This poor dog was fucked. So, I did what I knew to do as a nine-year-old. I ran.

Fear of witnessing death. Fear of helplessness. I ran without much direction through the woods, ignoring the thunder of twigs snapping beneath my feet. I ran like hell, halted at last by the sound of laughter.

My brother, Elliott, sat on a tree stump, his friends passing a hash pipe beside him. When I stumbled up, wheezing and sobbing and an obvious wreck, they laughed even harder.

"Elliott, please!" I took his hand, pulling at him. "Please! There's a dog and it's caught in a trap and—"

"Look, runt, I don't have time for your crap." He puffed out his chest, signaling the others to grunt in agreement. "We got things to do."

Yes, my brother was an asshole. But beneath that asshole-ish veneer, lurked a Delongchamp, and while Delongchamps might be world-class fuck-ups, we are not without conscience.

"Please, Elliott." I gave him the look. The "little Timmy has fallen into the well" look. The "little sister who saw you clean out of Dad's wallet and didn't tell" look.

"All right, all right!" He hitched up his jeans and growled. "Man, this better be good."

As predicted, Elliott didn't offer to bitch when he saw the dog. He stretched to break off a green oak branch. After successfully prying the trap from its leg, he sank to his knees to cradle her in his arms.

"I don't know what else we can do, runt." He spoke softly, tears coming to his eyes. "I...I can't..."

I was just a kid, and brother did I ever wail like a kid.

"WE CAN'T JUST LEAVE HER!"

"All right! All right! Christ!" Elliott was pissed, but not as much as he let on. Very carefully, very lovingly, he lifted the shit-covered dog and carried her back through the woods to our home. She lived to be gray. We named her "Trapper."

Gratefully half-stoned from a mild sedative, I had let my mind take me to a time of fewer complications. We'd had only one dog when I was growing up. The scent of sterile gauze freshly brought this to memory as a nurse taped an IV into place atop my hand.

"This city's going to kill you."

Chalk it up to post-natal hormones, severe lactose intolerance, or an allergy to non-off-the-rack clothing, but Faith had definitely gone around the bend after the baby was born. The quiet, gentle wife I had acquired shortly after her header into my front fence, had mutated into a woman seldom at ease. If I fretted over Banky, she did doubly so, and she had me, a bigger baby than Banky has ever been, to fret over as well.

God help her.

I closed my eyes and leaned back against the cool sheets.

Christ.

I was trapped.

"I'm serious, Macy." Faith shoved the now towel-wrapped dildo into her bloated tote bag. "This city's killing you."

And she was right, I suppose. I hadn't looked well in a while, even though I was technically in retirement and should have felt more relaxed. I hadn't had a tourist snap a quick pic of me at some tony café, thinking I was Sigourney Weaver dipping her dim sum into wasabi, for quite some time. Smog was a daily and often heated subject between us. Every tickle in my throat had to be the onset of germ warfare. People we saw every day weren't above suspicion. Three years after 9/11 and I still couldn't walk past a falafel stand without glancing over my shoulder.

"Let's just try and relax here, okay?" I reached for her hand. "I'm fine. I'll be fine." But I knew better. And she knew better. And she was a formidable force, indeed, when armed with hours of online research.

"Look, Macy, I've done my homework. The cleanest air in the world is in Tasmania." She grinned. "I'm not suggesting Tasmania. I checked, and they don't have a Saks."

"I suppose that's a relief."

"Philadelphia isn't bad."

"Ick!" I made a face, remembering a layover. "Uh-uh."

"Aspen?"

Dr. Todd entered. (I call him Dr. Todd as he'd introduced himself that way when I first arrived. Upon reading his I.D. badge, I saw that Todd was his *first* name.) "Actually," he said, "you might want to consider something warmer..." He glanced at my chart. "Says here that you came to the ER for your asthma three times last winter."

"On my fifth visit, I get a toaster oven."

He didn't crack a smile. Instead, he wrinkled his zitty brow. "Things like this don't get better, they get worse.

If I were you, I'd consider moving to a warmer, more arid climate."

But you're not me, Dr. Todd, with your Fisher-Price stethoscope and pimply chin.

I huffed. Meanwhile, Faith was eating this up. "You know, southern California's air rating has improved a lot over the last couple of years." She beamed. "Just think...Rodeo Drive, the ocean..."

Ah, yes, the ocean. I winced. *The ocean. The rain. The mudslides that once claimed a piece of land in Laguna Beach that I'd invested in, one I was still fighting the insurance company over.*

"I'll think about it." And I would. When I felt like it. My eyes darted from Faith to the door, and back to Faith. "Where's Banky?"

"With Lavinia and Mark." Faith leaned closer, serious. "You know, it really scares him when you're sick."

"He told you that?" I shrugged. "I always reassure him."

Dr. Todd put his pen in his pocket. "Children are remarkably perceptive, Mrs. Delongchamp."

"Being fresh off the teat yourself, you would know."

Dr. Todd left abruptly.

"Less than two minutes and you scared this one off. I believe that's the record." Faith laughed and pressed my hand. "Honey, I know you love New York. I know that this has been your home for a long time. But I'm worried. I want you healthy. I'm asking you to please..." She stroked my arm. "Think about this."

I was tired. I was a little weak. And she'd played the Banky card. So I caved. "Okay. You do some house hunting, set us up some appointments, and we'll have a look."

I still had the Band-Aid on my arm from having blood taken when we landed at LAX.

Perhaps, as with AA and psychotherapy, I'd learn to live in la-la land and buy a house, go along with things, and shut up about it. A tolerant existence. As with everything else, perhaps I should just take a deep breath, let it pass, and write out a check.

Chapter 3

I lay in the bold California sun, stretched out on a poolside chaise longue at the Beverly Hills Hotel. No crowd, thank you. In November, California types sheltered themselves from the brutal seventy-degree cold. I had the palms and the pool to myself.

Take a deep breath and...let it out.

I'd been in need of a rest—some warm weather time. We wouldn't really be moving here, of course, but if Faith had to shop for a house to feel satisfied, so be it. Me, I would relax and let her do the legwork. She'd taken the boy along with her, so my only companions were a glass of ice water...

"Flip me over, Girard. I believe I'm done on this side."

...a young man in a white sport coat ready to fulfill any whim I might have, and...

bleeeeeeep!

...my motherfucking cell phone. Constance. "Hello, Constance."

"Every night, it's the same dream."

I nodded, though of course she couldn't see this.

14

Oh, brother...

"I open the door and there's a big blue box on my front stoop. I check the card. It's for me. And I open it and find..."

A head.

"A head!" She began sobbing. "A head with a wig on it!"

It wasn't a pleasant visual, this head with a 'do askew.

"I guess just any old thing isn't more attractive if it comes in a Tiffany's box, after all." Pause. No laugh. Tough crowd, this Constance. "Honey, you're strong," I said lazily. "You truly are. You shall overcome."

I stood, stealthily pulling the bikini wedgie from my crack and bending toward the herbal jacuzzi, phone still in hand.

"What?" I held the cell toward the fizzing water. "I...I'm losing you...I..."

One flick of the thumb and I was free from the flip phone. For the time being.

Girard helped me slip my robe over my shoulders, and I slipped him a twenty, smiling.

Who needs a house? Maybe we could just live HERE.

Eyeing the hotel doors, I knew a few of the ghosts that dwelled within. Catherine Marks was one.

Ah, Cath. We hardly knew ye.

Catherine Marks, a sometime more than onetime movie and television producer, dead at fifty-three. Survived by ex-husband, Michael Marks. Catherine Marks had owned a Mercedes convertible back when it was actually the thing to own a Mercedes convertible. Before that, a DeLorean. With gullwings, no less. Blaring Nine Inch Nails through Hollywood Hills, our conversations had all been manic and one-sided, each of us screaming over the music and never hearing the other, laughing at the roar of noise and the seductive energy that the white powder had brought us both. I'd heard she'd graduated to freebase…and from the Benz to a Maserati.

Our last chance meeting was at the Polo Lounge a year or so back. She at the bar smoking, of course. Me with attorney and sans wifey, en route to eyeing some property just to keep myself in the real estate game. Her silver hair was no longer silver but white, so white, and she was pale. I'd known Cath to be up for days and look like a mint, tan and glistening spiked hair and smiles. Sitting alone at the Polo Lounge, though, she'd looked fragile and, well, old. We caught eyes for a moment that day, and looked away. Better to remain old friends than renewed friends, our eyes said. Better to remember how it was than to know how it is.

"Ms. Delongchamp?"

Remembering Catherine Marks had frozen me in my tracks. Girard stood before me, confused.

"Is there anything else I can help you with?"

"No…I…" A single tear had streamed down to meet my jaw line. I wiped it away and flipped myself over on the chaise. "No, thank you."

Take a deep breath and…let it out.

I closed my eyes. It was my part of the "thought-cleansing therapy" I'd subscribed to at Faith's behest.

Accept the moment for what it is, I thought. *And let it pass.*

Such random knowledge could have been derived much more cheaply by viewing old *Kung Fu* episodes. The wife, however, had signed me up with "La Shrink," a woman of forty with a gap in her teeth so wide you could flick quarters into her mouth from across the room. La Shrink wore knee-high leather boots along with her long black skirts, and had a smudging stick on her desk beside a teakwood incense holder.

It was like being counseled by Stevie Nicks.

A move to L.A. would keep me out of Stevie's reach, I pondered.

A move to L.A. would bring an end to Constance's constance.

It was a thought.

Chapter 4

Eager to act like tourists while Faith toured available homes, Banky and I cruised up Pacific Avenue, sunglasses on, at last reaching a Venice Beach parking area by mid-morning. Jim Morrison glowered down at us from his painted form on a building. I opted to pre-empt the inevitable inquisition and said, "See there, boy? That's Jim."

"Does he own Venice Beach?" Good question. Banky, already cruising real estate. That's my boy.

"Pretty much."

"Will he be at the beach?" Banky seemed not only interested in the shirtless icon, he seemed genuinely impressed. Even Donald Trump didn't own a whole beach. "Can I meet him?"

"Banky, if Jim Morrison is at the beach, I'll be happy to introduce you."

He grinned, staring out the windshield. "Cool."

I hadn't been to the boardwalk in years. It made no matter. Things hadn't changed, really. We'd barely made it from the parking lot when the Scientologists hit us up for a free intelligence test. These weren't the harmless, shorn-headed Krishnas of the 1970s. These people were far scarier. Each was dressed in low-level androgynous matching khakis and olive tops. Same belt, same shoes, same aggressively positive demeanor. And when I said "No, thank you," that wasn't enough. As we politely made our way past, I felt a hand on my arm.

"It'll only take a minute of your time..."

I swiveled, grabbing her/his/its wrist. "Fuck off, zealot. I said I wasn't interested." The young L. Ron pulled away, stunned. Enter Nobuzz, the ancient god of sobriety. Before, I'd have gotten a real giggle out of the situation, probably even played along, but not now. Nobuzz had no patience. Nobuzz now ruled me like Thor and his magic hammer.

We moved on and Banky asked, "What's a zealot, Mom?"

"A blind follower." I smirked.

"The people who go to church?" He kept walking, eyes straight ahead, already a master of the "walk and talk" that you learn by necessity in New York. My boy, already the big-city type, already one to anticipate the moves of people around him and navigate his way through a crowd. Already on the go.

"Not all of them, no." How could I put this? "Just the ones who use their religious beliefs as a basis to judge others."

"They think they're better just because they go to church, right?"

"Right." I was amazed. I wanted to slip him a fifty. Goddamn, kids are smart.

I bought bamboo mats for us to sit on and we had a picnic of greasy boardwalk fare: hamburgers, fries, funnel cakes, and a shish kabob of questionable ingredients. In a past life, I'm sure I was a 400-pound carny.

"We should have come earlier," I said, chewing a ball of food as I spoke. No pressure for etiquette in Banky's presence, thank you. "We could have watched the sun rise."

He and I had become sunrise junkies, of sorts (after the sun's initial appearance, I'd dip him in sixty SPF, of course). Things that are somewhat cliché as an adult haven't yet lost their luster to a child. Most mornings found me with my coffee on our rooftop patio, initially posing under the guise of reading the newspaper, succumbing to the inescapable urge to set aside the classifieds to watch him smile at the sun as it struggled up through the smog. Hearing tales of sullen teenagers on television talk shows, I scoffed. I enjoyed Banky for the moment, each day like it was our last together.

"What about the moon?" He had mustard on his face and stared out at the waves. In his profile, I could see the man he would become. He would be beautiful.

I started to explain that the moon doesn't rise, it just is, but I could tell Banky's concentration had moved on to more interesting things. He pushed a toy truck through the sand, covering it as he made windy sounds, uncovering it to load its bed with tiny shells.

The ugly thought crossed my mind, the nagging reality.

I'll be sixty-six when he graduates high school. I'll be carrying a defibrillator in my purse by then IF I'm alive at all...

Jolted from my moment of mortality by a long *bleeeeeep,* I was almost pleased that Constance was calling. Again. I flicked open my phone.

But it wasn't Constance, it was Faith, who had "incredible news." She'd found the perfect place for us, and wouldn't we like to meet her there ASAP?

Of course we would. Why waste our time watching the waves, stuffing ourselves, driving up to ride the Ferris wheel at the pier, holding hands, and buying stupid souvenir t-shirts and toys when we could be viewing real estate!

Now, normally, I would have been excited at the prospect of procuring new property, but this wasn't just a house, this was THE house. The house we'd eat in, revive our sex life in, lounge in, LIVE in.

Stuck onto the fringes of Santa Monica and the Pacific Palisades, Bel Air and the O.J.-notorious Brentwood, Rustic Canyon had a sophisticated rural flavor. A fair look around, and you see no obvious signs of class struggle: no "grandfathered" homes as in New York, no three-generation or rent-controlled dilapidated dwellings resting next to a sleek series of condos. There is no subway to bring publicists and prostitutes together in one urine-soaked stall. No, Rustic Canyon doesn't let the Jets and the Sharks come to mingle, thank you. Places like this allow the occasional figurative visitor's pass, but private police patrol the quiet streets. Unfamiliar and unwelcome faces are gently shooed away, or so you hope. As we pulled the car up front, I couldn't help but be reminded of the house in Hansel and Gretel: lovely and edible and oh-so-delicious.

I'd never been one for bedroom communities before. Piqua had been my sole suburban experience, and this whole scene looked to be nothing more than a pumped-up Piqua.

The estate in question had no gate, no buzzer to let you in. Obviously, no one worried about any newly re-cruited Manson family members straggling in to pose a slaughter. Massive spider webs linked the oak trees and crowned the shrubs and ferns. Webs seemed to end at the edges of the crumbling walkway, running up the mountain to a guest house and main house that couldn't be seen until we were almost standing inside of them. Thick palm trees and tropical flowers made up what may have once been a lawn, and the undeniable natural beauty, the sheer oxygen content of the place, was almost overwhelming.

According to our realtor's spiel, it had once been owned by a friend of John Wayne's, and the guest house had seen many a cavort between the Duke and a bevy of young Mexican beauties.

I ran my hand through my hair.

"Well?" Faith was ready to burst. And here I was: the stick pin to pop the bubble.

"It's alright," I said. I meant it. It *was* alright. Truly. It just wasn't, well…me.

Her shoulders dropped. "You don't like it."

But I did. How could I not? It was incredibly chic, se-cluded, safe. It was a place I never thought my life would unfold in, however, and it scared the hell out of me.

"Boy, it's big." Banky stood before the fireplace, which he could nearly walk into without ducking.

That it was. Big. Big and quiet. Where were the honking cars? The sirens? The garbage trucks? I thought we were moving to a *city*.

I moved out to the front deck that rose above the foliage enough to allow a view of the ocean, as well as the street below. I knew this place already. Everyone walks their dogs at the same time. The same kid on the skateboard, dragging a Jack Russell terrier. The bloodhound's owner, who's the only asshole in the neighborhood who dared to slap a George W. Bush sticker on his Range Rover. It's an endless loop tape running: the dog walkers retrieving poop in plastic bag-covered hands, the stroller-pushing nannies, the headphone-wearing housekeepers, the leaf-blowing gardeners, the sun-hatted retirees…and sooner or later, you stop varying your schedule and surrender to the parade yourself.

I took a deep breath of relatively clean air. Of course it was clean. Nobody smokes here. No one drives with their windows down, their radio blaring. Jamie Lee Curtis, a real, live movie star, lives just up the street, but you'd never know. No one treats her any differently than they do any other neighbor, and she, herself, extends the same safe and smiling nod any decent neighbor would offer if you pass on the street. Faced with the sight of Jamie Lee in her bathrobe fetching her newspaper at the curb, would I be able to resist a teenage squeal? Sure. And then I thought of the leggy lovely I'd tracked in most every film since her debut in *Halloween*, and my heart thumped. Sigh. Maybe not.

I felt the coolness of the deck rail beneath my sweaty palms. Sure, the rail was tall, but was it tall enough to dissuade a determined four-year-old from climbing up and over?

I glanced down at the swath of brick steps leading up to the house. I saw the wispy webs and wondered where those spiders were hiding. But the sunlight caught me there on the deck, warming me gently and comfortably all over until I felt a smile fight its way onto my face. I let my hands grasp the silver railing loosely, feeling the breeze catch my hair as I mused of potential holidays, parties, and candle-lit interludes. This wasn't just an apartment, it was a home. It had land and trees and mountains. It wasn't just a place to live, it had a life of its own, and offered a new one to us.

I licked my lips. I tasted salt from the ocean.

Maybe this wasn't such a bad place after all.

Chapter 5

After viewing our potential sanctuary in Santa Monica, back at our suite at the Beverly Hills Hotel, Faith and I lay hand-in-hand on our bed, each wearing a complimentary mud mask with cucumber-slice eye patches. A CD playing "Sounds of the Divine Spirit" (that Faith had scored from some mysterious friend in Topanga Canyon) had already lulled Banky into a coma in the next room. Faith seemed to be running a close second, a low, manly snore resonating from that hot little bod. As for me, I wasn't quite buying into this whole laid-back California thing just yet. I jiggled my foot beneath the covers. I grabbed a stick of gum from the nightstand and chewed it passionately. The "Divine Spirit" might have been soothing to the assorted flakes of the West Coast, but it grated on me like Garth Brooks. Popping my knuckles, craving my MP3, I considered the move.

What if this is a complete flop?
What if we hate it?
What if Faith loves it and I hate it?
What if Britney Spears moves in next door?

Simply sharing my insecurities with Faith would have been too simple. Instead, I started an argument.

I nudged her arm and the snoring stopped.

When I'd first come to New York, green and corn-fed with a decent bank account and little experience in the ways of the urban lesbian, I met a couple that took a bit of a fancy to me, and I to them. Their names were Kris and Betty, and they were a dandy couple: sophisti-cated, educated, intellectual, successful. What was miss-ing? A baby, or at least that's what Kris thought. A baby! It seemed silly to me, nothing but a wrench to throw into smoothly running works, but that's what they wanted...and how. So, one evening after a significant amount of Bacardi and Coke, I gave in. I offered them what they were lacking: a good egg.

"You offered them a piece of your body?!" Faith sat up abruptly, upon my confession. The "Divine Spirit" ceased its sounds.

"Well, now...it's not as if I was giving an actual baby away. Besides, I rather liked the idea of having a little me out there. I wish they would've accepted my offer, now that I think of it. I could have visited, watched it grow up..."

Laughing, she slapped my thigh.

"Leave it to you to skip childbirth and actually *RAISING* the child and still want all the perks."

I laughed. She had me pegged.

Faith reclined beside me. She waited a beat and then said sweetly, "Macy?"

"Yes?"

"Knowing what you know now about yourself, would you still have given them an egg?"

WTF?

"What I know about myself, now?" I felt my face flush beneath the mud, my hands begin to shake. I sat up and took the cuke slices from my eyes and threw them down like a gauntlet. "What the hell is that supposed to mean? It's not as if you're championship breeding stock!"

Faith sat up and threw down her cucumber gauntlet.

"At least I'm not an alcoholic and a sex addict!" She paused, cocking her head in mock thought. "Let me rephrase that...*FORMER* sex addict."

With a rageful grunt, I flew to the desk and sent the roses I'd bought for her the night before sailing across the room. In the second it took for that cheap vase to explode against the wall, I was no longer just an alcoholic former sex addict, I was a *violent* alcoholic former sex addict.

Lack of booze hadn't brought this on, I was convinced. It was marriage. Marriage had made me turn this wretched corner and spin out. Nobody wants to be the confirmed semi-invalid who's shuffled out west for health reasons. And on my own dime, no less.

"I saw you, you know." I moved toward her, looming over her, watching her shrink into the corner away from my shadow. "I saw you *fucking* yourself with my Henry Ford figurine."

"What?" Faith's face reddened.

"The one on my desk. The one you made me in that machine at Greenfield Village." I nodded. "I saw you masturbating with my little statue of Henry Ford. So don't be acting like you're Miss Polly Purebred, honey. I mean, I know I've let you down. I know you're hard up for a lay, but COME ON..."

"Macy." She eyed Banky's door. "I think we both better settle down."

"You didn't even use a condom!"

"MACY!"

I moved closer still. In this proximity, an eruption was inevitable. I didn't know if we were going to fight or fuck. Either way, I didn't feel particularly confident in the outcome.

Is she afraid of me?

I swallowed hard.

Am I afraid of me?

But when I caught her eyes with mine, the whole Henry Ford thing, well, it made us laugh, then hug.

"I'm sorry." It sounded so hollow, such a limp response, but what else could I say? Besides, I *was* sorry. Truly. And the laughter had taken away the momentum of my temper, but still...still, I didn't quite feel right about sticking around after such a scrap.

"I should go."

Grabbing at clothes, I hastily packed my valise.

Faith crouched, picking up glass and rose petals from the floor.

"I'll get another room." I lifted my bag and moved for the door. "If the real estate agent should be by with some papers in the morning, just send her my way."

"What?"

I sighed, defeated in the doorway. "I told her we'd take it."

And then I walked out, mud still on my face.

Chapter 6

I let myself sink into the deep water and suds. My new room was quiet, leaving me vulnerable to memory...

"Come on, honey! Let 'er rip!"

Faith grunted, clutching my hand so tightly I felt it crunch.

"I can't!"

How could she? I found myself preoccupied and pissed off that baby kangaroos are only a couple of inches long. They crawl out on their own and make their way up to the pouch.

Faith was huffing like a guppy on land. I kissed her forehead.

Why can't humans be marsupials? Why couldn't this kid just pop out of the pouch like a toaster pastry at nine months along?

"Come on, sweetheart! We're almost there! Push!"

After just an hour of labor, Banky's head blooped out from between Faith's legs like a flower from the ground. One look at this squalling blob and I was bawling right along with him. One look at Faith holding our baby and I wanted to shield them both from the world, shelter them from weather and war and, well, life.

One look at the afterbirth and *clunk!* I hit the floor, whacking my head on a steel table on my way down.

I spent the rest of Christmas morning passing out cigars and getting a cut above my eyebrow stitched. It was the happiest day of my life.

Chapter 7

I was feeling anxious, and there was only one way to fix it. An onsite masseuse at such an hour was too much to ask, even in Beverly Hills. After politely relaying my needs, my destination was whispered from concierge to driver and I was whisked off onto Sunset Boulevard. Motion sickness had never been much of a problem, but on this night I held my head in my hands, hiding my eyes from the headlights swimming by.

We pulled to the front of the lavender brick building. I took a seat inside, fingering a dangerous amount of cash in my jacket pocket. Faced with such a desperate mood only four years ago, this would have been a $1,200 evening, no problem. Drinks, tips, women. I'd taken the maximum out of the ATM machine out of habit.

But things had changed. Alone in the semi-dark room, I felt small, very small, in my chair against the wall. I recognized the music playing softly. Yes, "Songs of the Divine Spirit" had followed me from the hotel suite. The "Divine Spirit" was haunting me, but good.

Tam had poked her shaved head out into the lobby when she'd heard the substantial door chimes announce me. I call her "Tam," as that's what her white smock said in little red letters on her left chest. At first, I'd thought it was "Pam," but no, it was definitely "Tam." She was not a Pam.

"I'm sorry I left the door open," she called from another room. I heard a sink running. "We're closed."

Tam had a lot of earrings and the sort of arm-sleeve tattoos that make one look dirty. I'd have pegged her as a student auto mechanic or record-store clerk, not a masseuse, but this was Los Angeles. Every gas station clerk was studying Ingmar Bergman and having their tongues pierced; every dishwasher had a script to pitch.

My shoulders sagged. Shit. "Look, I'll pay you double. I'm just in an awfully bad way," I called back. "Please. I won't keep you long. I just need…"

Tam appeared beside me suddenly. "Some TLC?"

I jumped.

How had she gotten next to me? "Oh! I didn't see you." Maybe she was a leprechaun. A tattooed, shorn-headed leprechaun with four hundred earrings. "Yes. That would be nice."

Tam gave me the elevator eyes, perhaps wondering if I was actually worth skipping the vegan buffet special for.

"I'm serious about paying double." And I was, but I wasn't going to beg the shrimp for a rubdown. "But if you're too busy, I'll…"

"Just give me a sec to lock up." She'd already started fiddling with the door, her back to me.

The door read "Buddha Thourneburg, proprietor."

Buddha Thourneburg: more of a punch line than a name.

Tam took my hand in hers and led me toward the back. We entered a small room appointed nicely with a massage table, sink, and a shelf of oils. The only light was from a tray of candles. The room smelled faintly of jasmine.

"Where shall I put my..." She was already helping me take it off. The girl moved like she was on wheels. "...coat?"

In a blink, she'd maneuvered me onto the table. I sat on its edge. "Shouldn't I take off my clothes? Put on a towel?"

Tam guided my shoulders back, resting my neck on a firm pillow, my head in her hands. Strong hands. I closed my eyes.

Ohhhhhh...

"Any last requests before we begin?" I could hear the smile in her voice.

"Truthfully?" I sighed. "Turn off this fucking new age music, will you?"

She laughed. "Sure. The shop owner makes us play it." I heard a click. The drums and chants were replaced with...the theme from *Picnic*?

"This okay?"

I smiled. "Perfect."

I let my head loll in her hands. She moved from the base of my skull around to my jaw, pausing to sprinkle her hands with oil before moving up to my cheekbones and forehead.

"You have huge sinuses." She ran her thumbs over my eyebrows.

"Is that a compliment?" I laughed, nervous. "How can you tell?"

"Tam knows all, baby." I felt her unbuttoning my blouse. I let her. "Now, let's see what else we've got going on, here."

The bald wonder laid her wide palms beneath my shoulders, dragging them down. It hurt, and I moaned involuntarily.

"You could use a lymphatic drain."

"Couldn't we all? Why don't you change my oil while you're at it."

She looked up at me, not removing her hands. Big eyes. Dark eyes under thick, dark brows. "Funny."

And then, well, she reached beneath me and unhooked my bra.

"So, um…" I stared at the ceiling as the inspection continued, a little uncomfortable at becoming a little too comfortable. "Where's a person go to school for this sort of thing?"

Tam's hot hands cupped my breasts and I felt an old familiar tickle in my panties.

Who wants Jiffy Pop? Yes, I still had a working clitoris. It had been resurrected. No purchase necessary.

My bra flung on the floor, my blouse off, I now felt Tam undoing my belt.

I didn't stop her.

Instead I lay back and felt a woman touching me, actually getting me wet, for the first time in months.

When I came, I cried. I'd like to say it was out of guilt, but I'm not sure.

Tam washed her hands in the sink and I sat up, stunned.

"So, now..." I picked up my bra. "What do I owe you?"

She laughed and struck a match with her thumbnail, touching it to a Marlboro Red.

"I don't know, man. I'm just the cleaning lady."

Chapter 8

In the back of my limo, I was reminded of shrink sessions past.

"So...you slept with her." The steady, undulating tone was that of my therapist.

"I didn't sleep with her, Stevie." I never told her why I called her Stevie, and she never asked. "I fucked her."

This has to be the worst scented candle I've ever smelled.

"So you fucked her, this waitress." She took out her notepad.

"And how do you feel about that?"

Is it lavender? Sage?

"How did it feel? All you ever do is ask me how I feel about this, how I feel about that." I stood and paced. "What do you want me to do, lie? How the fuck do you think I feel about it?"

Is it cow shit that's burning on the fat little Buddha on her desk?

She peered over her licorice-red reading glasses. "Yucky?"

"Christ." I went to the window, considered jumping, and then remembered we were on the ground floor.

"I suppose the real question is: How does *Little* Macy feel about this?"

Ah, yes. My favorite strain of questioning. "Little Macy" was who she always wanted to talk with. How could I convince her that Little Macy had either run away or been sent to reform school a long time ago?

"There is no 'Little Macy.'" I ran my hand through my hair. "I'm six feet tall in my stocking feet, god-dammit. Besides, if *Little* Macy was even vaguely interested in fucking Shaquanda in the bathroom of the Traveler's Club and Tuba Museum, I'd be sending *her* to therapy, not me."

A pause.

Stevie reached out with a box of Kleenex.

This is what she called a breakthrough. Go, Stevie.

This is what I called guilt.

Chapter 9

Grace Foster, real estate agent and bearer of multiple facelift scars, dropped by earlier than I'd expected. After noting a few changes made via fax by my attorney, I took pen in hand, despite my infidelity hangover. Faith sat at the other end of the room, watching as I signed my name sixteen times. We agreed to rent until closing, speeding up the move.

As for the price, I'll put it to you this way: I could have bought half of the six-million-dollar man and a Bulgari wristwatch.

After receiving several bubbly congratulatory attempts, I ushered Grace Foster out and returned to perch on the edge of the sofa.

"Banky asleep still?" It wasn't quite eight in the morning.

She nodded.

"Nice house, isn't it?"

She smiled, slightly. "Yes."

Silence, then softly...

"Macy?"

"Mmm-hmm?"

"Can I ask you something?"

Shit. Did I look that guilty? Did I still have just-been-fucked hair?

"If it wasn't for Banky, would you have left me by now?"

I felt a cold shiver of surprised relief. "No!" Which wasn't entirely true. At our worst moments together, I'd wondered the same thing myself. "Why would you ask that?"

She crossed her ankles and squirmed. "Well, it's just that...I mean, you're good about taking your meds now, and we have a housekeeper." She looked at the floor, then back at me. "And you never want sex. Sometimes I feel like...I mean...what's the point of having me around?"

And here it came, the guilty realization: I'd neglected her. By being so attentive and devoted to Banky, I felt I'd been the same to Faith by proxy. Not so.

I clasped my hands, arms resting on my knees. I let our eyes meet.

Does she really think she's nothing to me?

"I want you around because"—my voice was breaking—"you're my girl."

Chapter 10

Ironically, Faith was in her fourth month of pregnancy and fertile as ever when I missed my period. The fifteenth rolled around and...poof! Nothing. Nada. The well had gone dry.

"Well, you're not pregnant!" My gynecologist, the comedienne.

"Looks like you're going through..."

And then the words came that would ring in my ears each day thereafter...

"...the change."

The change. It sounded so mysterious, so important, so...final.

"Thanks." I took my feet from the stirrups and sat in a daze.

"I...um...yeah. Thanks."

"If you experience any pain, any dryness or discomfort, any serious, you know..." She made circles with her finger beside her head. "...mood swings, just give us a call."

Doc was halfway out the door when I grabbed her by the shoulder.

"Germaine, am I..." I lowered my voice to a whisper. "Am I going to grow a beard?"

Germaine laughed. "No, Macy. Let's play this by ear, shall we?" She put her hand on my shoulder. "If need be, I can prescribe hormones. But until you notice some symptoms, we can hold off. It's not what it used to be. It's manageable."

Her tone had been comforting and confident. So why wasn't I confessing to the vaginal dryness? The mood issues? The whole hurricane that my life was becoming?

Because I was just plain scared.

Chapter 11

Gone, along with the smokestacks and steamer trunks, is the romance of train travel. Let it be said that in planning the trip, I had the best of intentions. The thought of riding aboard an art deco bullet as it ran like a ribbon throughout the countryside was, well, nostalgic and romantic. Vi Rogers, my step-mother and appliance saleswoman extraordinaire, had arrived on a train in my hometown of Piqua, Ohio, when I was seven. She'd descended the steps in slow motion, a movie star among the locals and rumpled passengers. She'd made her entrance into my life from a train, and I treasured that memory.

Vi had also killed a man on a train, the tale of which was told to me in drunken confidence. The act itself was clearly in self-defense (a bum sharing a boxcar tried to rape her, and she clubbed his head with a scrap piece of lumber). Her swift disposal of his body (rolling him off into a swamp) wasn't so much self-defense as self-preservation. Among hobos and regular rail riders, she had broken a code. Among the general populace, she'd broken a commandment and really rubbed it in.

I loved her for this. I loved the noir grittiness of it. Vi had the sleek, seedy good looks of a gangster's moll, and she'd actually had the nerve to whack somebody when necessary.

She'd been my first love.

It was all this black-and-white movie sentimentality that had made me convince Faith to take a train instead of flying or driving to spend Thanksgiving with her parents. Upon boarding, my sentimentality faded. Immediately.

Faith's parents, formerly runabout gypsy-types to be polite, formerly grifting swindlers to be truthful, had finally settled themselves in a Winnebago somewhere east of Phoenix. Armed with only our wits and an enormous frozen turkey packed in dry ice, we sallied forth on our journey via Amtrak, set to arrive four days before the holiday. Glancing about the train's interior, it was easy to see the results of the dwindling rail industry. Sparsely populated seats were covered in *Three's Company*-orange burlap, and there was a faint but general armpittish odor. Hardly the Ritz on rails. Even our first-class sleeper car was nothing more than our own private trailer park. After literally standing on the toilet to take a shower and straddling a bird for hours, I was ready to commune with Ma and Pa Littlefield in a semi-upright position.

"Tell me again why we don't just buy a turkey there," I said, feeling the lid of the Styrofoam cooler crunch beneath my resting feet. Faith must have heard, as she eyed the lid cautiously. "Well I've got to put my feet somewhere. The bird should be fine. Me, I might get cancer from this shit..."

"Tell me again why we took a train?" Faith laughed. "Macy, you're not going to get cancer from dry ice. And this turkey is organic. It's better for us. It's free-range."

"This thing leaks on me and I'll launch it out the exit." I lifted my ankle to check for burns. "Can't get much freer range than that."

The jostling and lengthy ride gave me a chance to consider my actions.

The Tam Incident.

Yeesh.

Other "incidents."

Ugh.

Certain things about these experiences rose and faded in my mind. Certain things about these infidelities were raw and clear and demanded a good stiff drink to muffle them. The AA alarm went off in my head.

Oh, no you don't.

I sighed.

Shit.

I searched my bag for an Alka-Seltzer and dropped the tablets into water. The dry drunk headache had begun to return.

Super.

I glanced down at the screen of my mobile. Nothing. No Constance. No anything.

Fuck.

Faith noticed my restlessness. "You okay?"

"Banky asleep?"

Faith patted my hand. "Yeah."

"You didn't see that conductor slip him a Benadryl or anything, did you?" I scanned the car for evidence.

"Because I've heard of them doing shit like that to, you know, keep kids subdued."

Faith rolled her eyes.

"Let's play a game!" I said it with enthusiasm, but quietly so as not to wake Banky, the only one small enough to stretch out and sleep. "Who has the most fucked-up family?"

"Oh, there's no contest." She was interested now and put down her magazine.

"Then you go first, big talker."

She began counting them off on her fingers. "Let me refresh your memory of my family tree. First, my mother had an affair with...get this...the ice cream man. Through this magical union I was conceived, and so my "dad" never treated me the same as the other kids."

She had me on the ice cream man. I wondered if her mother sometimes got weepy at the sound of "Old Mc-Donald" played over a loudspeaker. Still, I pressed. "Siblings?"

"Both sisters pregnant at sixteen. A brother just arrested for his third DUI." She folded her arms, gloating. "Beat that."

"I'll see your brother's DUI and raise you my brother's heroine problem and not one but TWO prison terms."

Her eyes widened. "Whoa."

"And lest we forget: bipolar birth mother who regularly ruminated about killing me and then herself. Alcoholic step-mother who slept with a guy with Mafia ties...she was my role model. Father who was always at his appliance store, when in reality he was out diddling whoever he chose..."

"Wait a minute. Hold it." Faith put up her hand. "Your father owned an appliance store?"

"Well...yeah." *Was it dysfunctional to own an appliance store? Kitschy, sure, but dysfunctional?*

Her face went white. "The only thing Marcus knew about his father was that he owned an appliance store."

My heart skipped. "Get out."

"I'm totally serious." And from her face, I could see she was, indeed, totally serious. "You think...?"

It had always been insinuated that Dad had scattered his seed throughout the tri-state area, and Michigan wasn't that far from Ohio.

I looked at Banky: quite tall for his age, wavy hair, strong jawline, signs of a propensity for fashion and entrepreneurship...all traits that neither Marcus nor Faith possessed. Was this nature or nurture? Was he my half-nephew, or my son? And had Faith slept with my half-brother?

My eyes darted from Banky to Faith, Faith to Banky. And then, in unison, she and I said: "I don't want to know."

Then, again in unison: "I'm glad you said that!"

"Jinx, buy me a Coke." I pointed at her and giggled.

Faith returned my nervous laugh. "So, how about we wind this game up?"

"Yeah, okay." I sighed. "Shoot."

She thought for a moment. "My uncle was a Patsy Cline impersonator."

I put my hands on my hips. "Prisoners would steal pigs and trade them for sex with my great aunt." I winked, sure of victory. "She was banished from her village."

"I bow to thee, oh great dysfunctional one." Faith conceded.

And for the rest of the train ride, neither of us slept, but neither of us talked, either. Instead, we hid behind newspapers and magazines.

Chapter 12

It preoccupied me, the whole-Banky-baby daddy thing. It wasn't inconceivable, the Marcus/Wild Bill Delongchamp equation. What if my son was really my nephew? It was all too hillbilly to grasp.

"Why, it's just lovely." I held up a knitted vest that had been presented to me by Faith's mother. It was royal blue with a red and white stripe running down the side, lending it a vintage *Star Trek* uniform quality.

"Try it on!" Faith nudged me.

"Oh, no." Her mother pshawed. "No, no. She doesn't have to do that."

"But she WANTS to." Faith nudged me, again. "Go on, Macy. Slip it on."

I'm not sure exactly what I felt for Faith, then. I can only suppose that it was akin to hate. Real hate. Fleeting, yes, but real. Fashion hate.

"Oh, sure!" I stood, hitting my head on the Winnebago's ceiling for the umpteenth time.

"Faith says you catch cold easily," Mama Littlefield said, smiling. "So I thought I'd make you a sweater."

Oh, God...why do you have to be so fucking nice? Why can't you be the total rip-off artist that I know you are?

The vest fit me like a tube sock, straight up and down and quite unflattering. I looked square, like an enormous Rock-'Em-Sock-'Em Robot. I looked ridiculous.

"It fits!" I sat down, already feeling sweat gathering in my pits.

"Thank you. Thank you so much. It's just lovely."

Mama Littlefield nodded, proud. "It sure does look nice. Faith, I have something for you. I didn't make it, but..."

She wandered off to what I assumed to be the bedroom. I snatched Faith by the arm.

"Thanks a whole fucking lot!" I joked.

"What?" She shrugged. "Is it so bad that you put on the sweater my mother made for you with her own arthritic hands? It means a lot that she made that for you, Macy. She's trying to accept us being together."

"It's as hot as a fucking bitch in this trailer and I'm dressed like a retarded Mork, Faith." I clenched my jaw. "I've drank enough cherry Kool-Aid to piss that Porta-Potty full, and I think I've got fleas!" I pressed my lips to her ear. "How could this get any worse?"

Of course, at that point, I hadn't met her daddy.

Chapter 13

Trish's and Hal's place was a lovely brownstone not far from my own abode. The down payment was a wedding gift from Hal's parents, and the subsequent (and necessary) structural renovation was his parents' way of congratulating him on his graduation from dental school. For all the rest, the doilies, designing, and accompanying accoutrements, they had only themselves to blame.

I awoke there face down in what looked like vomit, but was strangely softer and smelled much more flowery.

Just stay still, I told myself. *Maybe this is how it felt for Jimi Hendrix. Maybe death is sweaty hair, a throbbing eye, and a Laura Ashley pillow.*

And then, the whispering voices...

Brittany: This is like that Morton Downey, Jr. guy.

Kate: Shut the hell up! And besides, it was ROBERT Downey, Jr. Duh!

Brittany: Shut up, yourself. Like you're all sophisticated now that you're taking a few classes at the junior college. Big shit.

A pause.

Brittany: She must have *reeeeally* been on a bender.

Kate: She doesn't drink anymore, retard.

Brittany: Think she'll remember how she got the shiner? (punch) OW!

Ah, the voices of angels. I must be dead. But the question is: Is this heaven or hell?

"Macy!"

"Girls, leave your Aunt Macy alone, now." It was my best friend, Trish. She moved closer to the bed, looking concerned yet jovial. "I take it you don't remember coming in yesterday morning, princess?" She laughed. "You were crying. You kissed my hand and said you'd been persecuted. Then you passed out and Hal carried you upstairs. And *that* was something to see."

Persecuted? Better that than prosecuted. "I'm sorry. I wasn't drunk, I swear."

"You were exhausted. Anyone would be after driving thirty-seven hours straight. Not the smartest decision you've ever made, though it's not been the worst." She felt my forehead. "I called Germaine. She stopped by last night and gave you an inspection and a shot of B12."

Ah. That would explain why my left butt cheek feels like a cannon ball.

Trish pulled the blanket up under my chin. "You snored like an espresso machine."

"The whole place was made of concrete blocks. I feel like my head's filled with peanut butter from breathing all that mold." I stretched. "How long have I been out?"

"About fourteen hours. Happy Thanksgiving." She buttoned the top button of my pajamas, which were obviously Hal's, as my arms shot out four inches from the cuff and the bottoms were like bad capris. "I checked for a pulse now and then, just to make sure we didn't have to call the medical examiner, but I let you sleep. Apparently, you needed the rest."

I plucked at the sweaty pajama top and grimaced. "And apparently, now I'm a tad ripe. Did Faith call?"

"No, but I didn't check your cell for missed calls. Want me to have the girls bring it up?"

"No. That's alright." *Unbelievable.* I frowned. "I don't suppose I should expect her to be concerned."

"You two get into it or something?" She touched my cheekbone. I winced. "Don't tell me she's responsible for this, because if she is, Macy…"

"I'm not a battered wife, Trish." I sat up and Trish produced an ice pack, touching it gingerly against my swollen eye. "You're a good mother."

"I've had a lot of practice." She pushed me back, pulling the covers up to my chin, again. "So, the black eye…"

Oh, God. Faith's father. Banky. And that god-awful lamp. "Let's just say you should see the other guy." I sat up again, shivering. *Why hadn't she called?* "I fucking froze half to death in the county lockup. I'm STILL cold. And she doesn't have the decency to even call."

It's not like I hit HER with the lamp.

"Jail?" Trish whispered emphatically, then backed up, easing the door closed behind her. "Uh…jail?"

"Uh…yeah." I blew my nose with a mighty honk. The peanut butter budged a tad. "I always thought it would be more, I don't know…clean, for one. And filled with horny women in tight jumpsuits." I honked, again, rolling my eyes. "None of the above."

"You arrived in a very ugly sweater."

"Ha!" I flounced. "Tell me about it."

Trish stepped back and poked her head into the hall. "Girls! Get your Aunt Macy some hot tea!" Obviously intrigued, she skipped the chair this time and sat directly beside me on the bed. "You mean you were actually in fucking JAIL?" She looked around, as if checking for the cops, then eyed me again. "Was it a DUI?"

"Absolutely not!"

"Of course not. You poor thing." She draped another blanket around my shoulders and patted my hand. "So, how did it happen? Are you going to be on Court TV?"

The door popped open behind us. A hand wearing Brittany's Swatch watch stuck a steaming cup in through the crack and said, "Are you in the Mafia?" before Trish slammed it shut. "Damn it, Britt, let us have a little privacy, here!"

A pause, then a muffled "Well, is she?" from out in the hall.

"Downstairs, Brittany Elizabeth! Now!" She handed me the tea. "Sip this." She kissed my forehead. "Poor baby. I just want the scoop. What gives?"

So I told her. I told her how Faith's father had grabbed Banky by his chubby little arm, grabbed him hard enough to leave a mark, in anger. I told her how I'd told him not to lay a finger on my boy, motherfucker, and how PTOOEY...I'd felt a wet loogey splat against my forehead from his nasty little puckered mouth...

I told her how I'd recoiled from his salivary assault, swinging my arm up to grab the hanging swag lamp with its translucent orange glass globe and... crash...brought it down onto his head.

"It was a tacky lamp. No great loss." I shrugged. "It was a mercy killing. The thing had to have come with the Winnebago. In, say, 1976."

"The goddamned cops banged my head onto the hood of their squad car. Look!" I pointed to my swollen eye. "They had me arrested for assault! Can you believe it?"

"With a tacky weapon?" She laughed. "Macy, I had no idea you were capable of such…"

"Violence?" I huffed. "He grabbed the boy! And he fucking spit in my face, the little prick! And I didn't really mean to hurt anyone. It all just happened so fast." I sighed. "Besides, after letting me freeze all night in that place, Faith finally came in with her parents and they dropped the charges. After I gave them a check."

"How much?"

"Forty-seven thousand dollars. A grand for every stitch in his scalp. I had my attorney Max write up a contract and fax it to the jail. It's not as if these are honorable people."

Cold cement floors, a faint pissy smell. Jail had been littered with snaggle-toothed crack whores and a pair of *Girls Gone Wild* drunken bar brawlers.

I pulled the ice pack away and let my eyes wander the ceiling. Yep, still had the floating spots. Great. Goddamned Nazi savage police. "I need to take a shower. I need to wash the white trash out of my hair."

But what I really needed was my wife, to hold me and rub my back and, yes, kiss my forehead. Lovely wife, who would have never left me stranded to shiver in a damp jail, who would have never condoned, let alone negotiated, any payola to her fucking gypsy-assed parents.

Lovely wife, who used to put out on a regular basis and read to me in bed.

"There's a robe on the back of the door in the bathroom. Plenty of clean towels on the shelf." Trish squeezed my hand. "Go get clean. Pretty up for dinner."

Safely across the hall, door closed, I peeled off Hal's pajamas and lifted the white robe from its hook. In my haze, I thought I felt steam, thought I heard giggles.

I spun around.

Oh, fuck.

"Kate!" I scrambled for the robe. "Jesus! Shit!"

But it wasn't just Kate. It was...

"This is Jackie Krepps."

...Jackie Krepps. A girl. Naked. With Trish's daughter. In the tub.

Naked!

Miss Krepps extended a sudsy hand. I turned my head, marching dutifully to the tub to shake it.

"Girls...Kate...I'm sorry." I kept my head turned, stepping back. *Christ.*

"It's okay" Kate smiled. "We can get out if you need to use the tub."

"Or you can join us," chirped Kate's lovely companion, clad only in her puka shell necklace.

More giggling.

Oh, God. Oh, this was far beyond even me. Even the OLD me.

And then came the knock at the door.

"Mace?" *Trish!*

My voice cracked. "Yeah?"

"Need anything?"

"No." I threw my finger to my lips to make them hush. "I believe I have more than everything I need right here."

Trish. Helpful. Innocent. Little did she know...

"Okay."

Kate and her concubine were crawling from the tub, the former more discreetly than the latter.

"Need us to do your back?"

Oh, this Krepps girl was getting on my nerves.

"Scram!"

By dinnertime, I'd managed to slap a little face powder on my bulging eye.

"I think you should wear a patch." Kate was chipper.

"That would be hot." Miss Krepps, always ready with her two cents.

Trish grabbed Hal's hand and stood. "Well, since none of us are religious, we can skip the whole traditional Thanksgiving prayer crap. But maybe we can go around the table and share something that we're thankful for." Trish raised her glass. "I'm thankful for being cancer-free for five years!" We applauded and hooted. "I'm thankful for my odd but somehow endearing family. And last but not least, I'm thankful for our surprise guest." She nodded at me and smiled. "Next."

"Well..." *I'm thankful for no longer being in the pokey or in that crummy RV.* "I'm thankful to be lucky enough to be in the company of dear friends, for no longer being a drunkard, and for the Prada fall collection."

As it neared Kate's turn, I could see her gearing up.

Oh, no.

She rose, and I saw that she was holding hands with Jackie.

"Kate." I said it as nonchalantly as possible, considering. "Think."

Trish shot me a confused look.

I sighed and stared at the turkey. *Que sera sera.*

Kate cleared her throat, smiling. I knew that smile. That was the patented "I'm here, I'm queer, get used to it!" smile.

Oh, no. No, no, no. Not the right time to do this...

"I'm thankful to have such a loving family..."

Here we go...

"...who I know will be happy for me when I introduce them to my girlfriend, Jackie."

Trish shrugged. "Honey, don't you remember? You introduced her when you came in."

"Trish ..." I touched her arm and leaned close. "Trish. They're not friends. They're girlfriends."

Her face fell. "You're kidding."

I shook my head. "I'm not kidding."

As if to punctuate my point, Kate pulled Jackie to her feet and they kissed. A big kiss. A wet kiss. A tongue kiss. A loooooong kiss.

Hal was stunned, frozen with carving knife and fork in hand.

"Well!" He smiled. "Let's eat!"

Chapter 14

Jon Secada stared down at us from a catwalk balcony.

"That guy's creeping me out." I shifted in my seat, whispering to Faith. "I'm sorry, I know he's a Grammy winner and all, but I don't like how he keeps looking at us. Maybe it's the lipstick."

"Maybe it's the red glittery nipples." Faith smirked. "Anyway, we're supposed to be looking at the stage, not at him."

"Well he's not supposed to leer at us. HEAR THAT, JON SECADA?"

Hearing me or not, he turned away, and I was grateful.

Faith looked confused. "This isn't like the *Cabaret* I saw when I was little."

"It's the dirty version." I yawned. "Some big-shit director's doing the farewell performances. That's why the fruit plate was forty dollars."

I plucked a shriveled grape from the plate on our table and whipped it upward, missing him only by inches. "That'll get him out of the rafters."

"You're going to get us kicked out of here!" Faith punched me playfully.

"Wouldn't be the first time."

"What are you talking about?"

I slid my arm around her shoulders. "Sweetheart, I was kicked out of this place before you were even born."

And it was true. I had been kicked out. Twenty-eight years before.

"Kicked out of a theatre?"

"Kicked out of a nightclub." I leaned back in my seat. "This used to be Studio 54, the wildest of wild New York nightlife."

Faith seemed impressed. "And you were kicked out?"

"For passing out halfway through the bathroom door." I nodded to my right. "Had my skirt hiked up and my hoo-hoo hanging out."

"My God, Macy!" Faith grabbed my arm. "What the hell were you on that night?"

"I don't know. Quaaludes. Vodka." I shrugged. "Whatever the mood demanded."

Faith turned her attention back to the stage before us, shaking her head. "It's a wonder you're alive."

"And home in bed every night before ten." I snuggled close to her and popped my gum. "You want another cranberry juice?"

"No, thanks."

"Your feet okay? Do you need to put them up?" Faith's ankles had been swelling since the second month of her pregnancy.

"I'm good." She smiled. "Hey, didn't John Stamos do *Cabaret* before?"

"I think he was the one before Jon Secada." I watched a prostitute play the accordion onstage. "Strangely, I'm glad we have Jon Secada for this performance. John Stamos is such a wannabe fag."

Faith laughed. "You weren't a fan of *Full House*, I take it?"

"The only thing good that came out of that show were those emaciated Olsens. Besides, John Stamos still has a mullet."

She laughed again. "Macy?"

"Yeah?"

"You've really been taking good care of me."

"Yeah, well…" I smiled.

"I'm afraid to have this baby." She leaned on my shoulder. "I've never done this before, and I've heard labor can last for days."

"Honey, we saw the film." I patted her hand. "That kid popped out of her in a snap. It won't be that hard."

"You don't think?"

"Nah. And I'll be right there, demanding pain pills."

"I don't want to take anything that could hurt the baby," she cautioned.

I kissed her cheek. "Oh, I don't mean for you. I mean for me."

So there we sat, bored at one of the farewell performances of *Cabaret*. A performance without Liza, a performance not even in a theatre, a grand performance by me.

I was scared as hell about the birth thing, too.

Chapter 15

"I don't believe it." Trish's eyes were glassy.

I sat across from her at the now vacant dining room table. Dishes cleared, now we had time to talk. I patted her hand and held onto it softly, noticing how tiny it was compared to mine. "Believe it."

"I'm serious. I don't believe it." She glared at me. "I refuse to believe it. It's just a phase."

"Trish, stop being your mother." I reached across, putting my hand on hers. "Remember when she told me I was going through a phase?" I patted her hand. "It's not a phase."

"I just don't get it." She looked lost. "I mean you, with your shitty upbringing, I can understand...but Kate's had it all so easy..."

"Being gay isn't a *side effect*. Come on, you know that!" I chuckled. "It's just part of who you are."

Trish pulled back, repulsed. "Well, it's not part of who I am, OR who her father is."

And the walls went up. It was one thing to have a friend who was queer. It was another to have a child who hops the fence. Being liberal was easy until it hit too close to home.

61

"Oh, fuck you." *Just get up and get of here, idiot, before this gets ugly.* "How shall you be fucked? Let me count the ways." I started to stand.

Trish grabbed my wrist. "Did you know about this and not tell me?"

"She begged me not to." I couldn't lie. "Now, take your mitts off me."

"Oh, my God!" Trish let loose of my hand, her mouth hanging open. "You *knew* this and didn't *tell me*?"

"She wanted to tell you and Hal on her own..."

"Well, she sure did!" Trish laughed, thoroughly pissed. "She sure as hell told us, didn't she? Right at the fucking family Thanksgiving dinner table!"

I had to agree with her there. "Not the best timing, no." I smiled. "But at least she was proud of herself and who she is. She didn't come crawling to you."

"Macy, you don't get it." She was locked in on my face now, not looking away for a second. "I want a *future* for my kids. I want to see them graduate college, get married, have a family..."

"Being a lesbian won't stop her. Look at Hillary Clinton, for chrissakes." I jerked my skirt straight. "And besides, why fix it if it ain't broke? Kate seems pretty happy."

"Oh, she is for now. You were happy at her age, too. Healthy, confident, proud. The most beautiful girl in our school." She pointed at me and the invasiveness of it made me flinch, made my neck get hot. "But look at you now."

Run. This is going to a bad place. This is your best friend of how many years? Run.

"Again, fuck you, but thanks for dinner." I turned to go upstairs and retrieve my coat. "I'll call you later."

"Oh, you're doing just great." She huffed out a laugh. "By the time she's through, that girl will have bilked you out of every dime you've got."

I knew it. I knew she would go there.

"Trish." I shut my eyes. I saw red. "Stop."

"I'm sure that Kate thinks you have this great, jet-setting life. I'm sure that's pretty seductive to an eighteen-year-old." She was really on one, now. "Truth be known, you wore yourself out whoring around and now you've settled down with a con artist."

A voice came out of me, deep and strong. I stood still and poised. "Don't talk that way about my wife."

"Are you *threatening* me?"

I stepped up to the table and slammed my hands down hard in front of her. "Take it however you like." The words came out like a growl.

"Fine." She shrank down a bit. "Just go."

And as I stalked out into the hall, I heard her yell after me: "Maybe Faith was right! Maybe you *have* gone nuts without the booze!"

I had nowhere to go but the apartment. I'd asked Lavinia if she could let in the movers and most everything was in boxes or disassembled and wrapped. No lamps, no chairs, no books, no bed. Life as I knew it was now in storage purgatory.

My coat wrapped about me, I slid down into a corner by the front windows and imagined someone holding me. Alone had never felt so, well, alone.

Chapter 16

"Get lost!" I whipped a stick at Karen Byrd, fifth-grade nemesis of Trish and, thus, nemesis of me.

"Aw, go play with yourself!" she retorted, floating on an innertube at Prater Pond, smiling with those buck teeth of hers jutting out. Thinking she was out of our range of thrown rocks, twigs, and whatever other elements, Karen Byrd then did the dirtiest deed one could do in the fifth grade: She flipped us off.

"That shit!" I looked at Trish, who was equally appalled. Simultaneously, we fished bottle caps, pull tabs, larger rocks, and hunks of rotted wood from the gravel piled along the railroad tracks. This was serious, goddammit.

In rapid fire, we launched our arsenal against Karen and her distantly floating innertube with no obvious success.

"Shit!" I'd always had a shitty arm. I threw like a girl because, well, I was one. "One of us should swim out and knock her off. That'll show her."

So went the plan. Trish took her awkward strokes out and disappeared beneath the murk before reaching Karen, intending to capsize the inner tube. But as I knew, and as surely Trish knew, there were drop-offs in the pond's floor. Before Trish could flip Karen from her floating perch, Trish had sunk below the surface, herself.

"Trish!"

My friend was gone. Oh, my God! I tore into the water, not bothering to remove my shoes or anything else. Goddamn that Karen Byrd!

"TRISH!"

By this time, Karen was giving quite a panicked search, herself, half-clutching her innertube. I dove toward Karen's knees, the grit hitting my eyes as I searched and searched. Finally, there she was. Trish! I yanked her to the surface, one-arming us both to the shore.

"Trish!" I turned her onto her side and slapped her back. Water shot out of her mouth and she choked, struggling to sit up.

I started crying and put my arms around her. Karen was intrigued.

"Did your life flash before your eyes?" She wondered. "Did you crap yourself?"

I slugged at Karen and tightened my hold on Trish.

"Don't ever leave me." I rocked her against me. "Please, Trish. Please don't ever leave."

Her father had once had to take a position out of town, and the threat of moving away had been there but we'd lucked out.

"I won't." She was crying, too. We shivered together. "I won't leave you, Macy."

Chapter 17

I spent the night in a classic New York manner: fetal, snoring, atop a stack of several unassembled boxes. All I needed was the sidewalk beneath me and a sign that read: "Homeless and Hungry" or "Homeless with AIDS," my favorite.

Technically, I *was* homeless. The house in California wouldn't be entirely readied for our arrival for another two days. The apartment was packaged and duct-taped thoroughly, even the drawers removed from the chest in my bedroom.

The chest in my bedroom. Shit!

As cavalier as I'd been with its placement at my office (bottom drawer on the right, beneath bottle of emergency vodka), I'd been paranoid, just a smidgen, about my coke stash at home. This had been such a powerful smidgen that I'd purchased a chest with a false bottom that locked...get this...with a magnet. Housed in what looked like a tiny white plastic chef's hat (*why?*), said magnet would unlock the hidden compartment when passed slowly over the floor of the chest. One soft *cah-lick* and you were in business, ready to pop open the hidden-hinged space that was roughly the size of a box of Phillie Blunts.

God only knows how much dope I have stored away.

And, out of habit...

Is the shelf life of coke virtually infinite, like that of a Twinkie? I wonder if it's still good?

I sighed.

A twinge of resentment poked at my flesh in prickly little shocks: I'd become such a bore. Whose idea was it for me to get off the stuff in the first place? The doctors? Faith? Me?

Ha! I don't think so. Not me. I wouldn't be smart enough to quit the shit on my own.

Or stupid enough.

And now I was trapped. I desperately needed my hair done. I wore practical clothing. I had an AA sponsor.

I'd become the very ilk I'd mocked for years.

Hands trembling, I ran the tiny chef's hat over the floor of the chest.

Cah-lick.

There before me lay the grail.

Thar she blows!

I spied with my little eye quite a little sack of coke alongside what was once referred to as a "dime bag" of marijuana. I felt the rush, the inadvertent smile.

I thought of my life *then*, and of my life *now*.

"Borrrrring," I said aloud, rolling my R's. "Borrrring. Borrrring. Borrrring."

Everyone had setbacks. Why, a slip-up would be entirely understandable, considering the circumstances. I mean, I was being uprooted from my home of, what, thirty-four years?

I felt unsettled. I felt angry.

It's not fair, goddammit. What does Faith have to sacrifice? A minimum-wage job? A futon in some basement apartment? A string of low-level executives to have one-nighters with? A diet of canned spaghetti?

With a primal grunt, I grabbed at the drugs and remained on my knees.

But wait…something else was in the secret dresser safe.

Ah, the gun.

Bro Elliott's gun.

A .38 Special with, surprise, the numbers filed off. Small but weighty. Undoubtedly hot. During one of his stints in the juvenile hall, I'd swiped it from my asshole brother's bedroom and failed to ever return it.

Why?

I remembered packing it when I left Ohio for the big city. I remember thinking I might need it someday.

Why?

Maybe I'd need it to protect myself.

Don't kid yourself, honey.

Or maybe I'd kept it around, like a spy or soldier with cyanide capsules, for when the enemies had captured me.

I sat down, my knees bent nearly to my chest, the gun dangling limply from my right hand. A very Mildred Pierce moment.

I eyed the drugs on the floor.

You got your chocolate in my peanut butter!

I eyed the pistol hanging in my hand.

You got your peanut butter on my chocolate!

Either path and my life was kaput. With the drugs, I'd never see Faith or Banky again. She'd never understand a colossal relapse. I'd never stand a stay at Betty Ford.

And sure, taking a bullet might end my boring existence, but what if the radical religious right was, well, *right*? What if their selective interpretations of Leviticus were legit?

I'd once dreamt of the devil: ten feet tall, bearded, stinky, scaly, with huge curled horns, and a tail. I'd hid from him underneath a table at the Piqua Elks Lodge.

I'd dreamt this when I was ten, and it hadn't left my memory.

I laughed out loud.

Even I was falling prey to the president's unholy propaganda.

Great.

As for the drugs, I whistled "Taps" as I poured them into the toilet and flushed.

Chapter 18

"This is an intimate piece of work," the green-haired scribe in a sleeveless Iron Maiden t-shirt said, motioning for everyone to move closer. "Could you all just...come forward a little."

So continued "Literary Night" at Meow Mix, a wry little dump in a section of town that made even cab drivers nervous. I'd peeled myself off the boxes in my apartment to come there in search of something: Companionship? Dirt under my fingernails? Five-dollar Cokes? Yes, yes. All that and more.

"And then...my sister and me...for that's what I called us...never 'my sister and I'...always my sister and me..." the faux-hawked rocker squawked. "We..."

"Oh, let me guess," I said, louder than I'd meant to say. "You fucked each other. You and your sister finger-fucked each other." Some gasped, some giggled. Either way, I had the crowd's attention, and attention, I suppose, is what I was in need of at the moment. "And now we're all supposed to think 'Oh, so that's why she's so "alternative"...so wild and wacky in her Doc Martens and "Jesus Is My Homeboy" belt buckle.'" I rolled my eyes, sitting back on my stool. "Gimme a break."

Wow! This is like being drunk without actually being drunk!

"Somebody get the bouncer," said a voice behind the bar, and suddenly a not-so-big butch had me by the elbow.

"Unhand me, knave." I put my free hand over hers and squeezed...hard. "Look, sister, you don't know what I've just been through. Let's just say that I'm a little stressed. So get your fucking little black-finger-nail-polished fingers off me before I call a lawyer, *capice*?"

Frightened, confused, or just plain bored, she released my elbow. I moved for the door and stood on a crate. "Anybody sick of this sideshow, you can meet me at Pete's!"

Surprisingly, perhaps an hour later, three gals took me up on my offer, and I took them up on theirs. I stayed straight, but they feasted on poppers and coke and came down with a joint. Late in the evening, darkness found me ensnared by a tangle of arms and legs, thoroughly exhausted and quite unsure of where I was.

Chapter 19

Faith had called my mobile six times. I noted this, sitting in a chair at Verona, a salon on the Upper East Side. My regular hairdresser hadn't been available for walk-ins. I took Brian, the new girl, and spilled to him about Trish.

"Pardon my French, sugar, but what a *cunt*!" He felt my pain, as all hairdressers do. "She did NOT need to get on your ass. Like it's your fault her little girl's a koala."

I jerked my head away from his scissors. "A *what*?"

"A koala." He leaned in and whispered, "One who eats bushes and leaves."

Ha!

By the time I left, I felt a bit haughty. Fresh cut, fresh dye job, fresh shellac on the nails. Yessirree, one quick trip to Barney's and I'd be my old self again. More or less.

I'd dialed Faith's cell in the cab. "Happy belated Thanksgiving, darling."

"Macy, where the hell are you?"

I preened in the mirror of my compact. *God, I'm a*

good-looking woman. She is sooo lucky to have me.
"I'm in New York, of course."

She exhaled. "Why didn't you call me back?"

Truthfully, I'd shut the ringer off, so I said, "The battery was dead and I left the charger at your parents'. Had to borrow one of Trish's." I smiled. "Sorry."

"Jesus, Macy, I was scared to death!" *Good!* "So you had dinner at Trish and Hal's?"

"Yes." I smirked. "It was no paper plates in the Winnebago with the in-laws, but it was pleasant enough. How's your father's noggin? Bet he could buy a lot of Aspirin with forty-seven grand."

"They were going to sue you, you know. For a lot more than forty-seven thousand dollars," she said. "You shouldn't have hit him like that, Macy."

"No shit." I slipped on my sunglasses. "I should have hit him harder."

"So, how are you and Banky?"

"We're okay." I paused, then softly... "We miss you."

I felt my stiffened resolve to be a hardass unstiffen. *Sigh.* "I...um...I miss you, too."

And Christ, I started to cry. "I'm sorry!"

"I know."

"I'm really sorry." I was actually *whining.* God, was I six years old? "I didn't mean...I didn't mean to hurt anyone." *Neither did Frankenstein's monster.* "Not your father or you. I..." I was sobbing, now, really wailing and letting loose. "God, I don't know what's happening to me!"

"It's alright. It's alright," she soothed, but I knew she thought differently. Faith had told Trish, her friends, probably the butcher, of how I'd changed since going cold turkey. She was a little afraid of me, and I didn't blame her.

I was a little afraid of me, too.

Chapter 20

I don't believe in psychics. I think it's a load of shit. This is precisely why I was so alarmed when I heard (insert overused *Twilight Zone* theme here) The Voice.

"Hey, kid."

A husky voice. A woman's voice.

I was in mid-piss at a stall in the ladies' room at Barney's when my step-mother knocked on the door. My *long deceased* step-mother, Vi.

The voice sounded just a touch higher than I'd remembered, but fuck, it *had* been over thirty years. And, well, one's voice was bound to change a little in the afterlife.

"Kid?"

She knocked again.

I'd better answer and be damned polite about it! "Yes?"

"Don't be afraid. Come on out." She laughed. "Let's get a look at you."

I looked down. Having shed my old clothes and stashed them in a shopping bag, I'd made a good selection, one she'd approve of. New suit, blouse, new stockings, new shoes. One could never go wrong with Armani, right?

Right?!

"Just a minute!" I said sweetly, crouching and trying to peer through the crack in the door. No luck.

"Come on, kid." The voice, it sounded a bit impatient...even testy. *Shit!* "Let's not take all day."

Who knew that hell would seem so much like Barney's?

"Look, I'm..." Might as well be honest. "I'm afraid."

"Oh, honey, don't be. I just want to have a look." The voice was soft now. Gentle and seductive, as I'd remembered. "Come on out and let Mother see you."

See me and what? Eat my brains? Rattle your chains? Show me Christmas past?

Still crouched, I laid my cheek against the cool metal door, panting.

"Now you're getting all worked up over nothing. Do you have your inhaler in there with you?"

God, it *was* Vi. Only her spirit would know, would be concerned, about my asthma!

I curled my fingers over the top of the stall, eyes closed as I poked my head halfway over the door, a petrified Kilroy.

It wasn't my step-mother. It wasn't Vi at all. It was some short and stubby little thing looking for...

"Becky?"

Becky?!

I was shaken. Happily shaken, but shaken. "Huh?"

"Oh, my goodness, I'm so sorry!" She giggled, embarrassed. "She wasn't in the dressing room, and I thought..." More giggling. "I thought you were my daughter!"

I popped open the stall door and stepped out, a good foot taller than her.

"And I thought you were my step-mother!"

We giggled together. I tried not to show the incredible relief I was feeling.

She composed herself to make polite conversation. "So, you're shopping with your mother, too?"

"No. Oh, no!" My shoulders still bounced, tears coming down my cheeks. "She's dead!"

My shoulders bounced uncontrollably. I simply couldn't stop. I kept laughing until long after she left, which she did, and in great haste, the poor thing. I suppose she ran off to report some well-dressed lunatic lurking in the bathroom.

"Oh, brother." I splashed cold water on the back of my neck and applied some lipstick.

It's okay. You're fine. It's just been a bad week, that's all. Everything will be fine. No ghosts, no hallucinations, no devil at the Elks Lodge.

Looking at my reflection, I realized my relief was tempered with...disappointment?

Maybe I'd wanted it to be Vi.

Vi, worm food or not, would never take shit like this. No, sir.

I smiled.

Vi would have kicked Faith's father's ass with no remorse.

I chuckled. I missed her.

Chapter 21

The day after Thanksgiving and the airports were clogged. I'd lucked into a cancellation, and yes, the eggnog was already flowing. I raised an eyebrow as the passenger beside me, studying a copy of *The Living Bible*, accepted a cup.

Should I ask if it's virgin?

I raised an eyebrow, spying as she sipped.

Is it really considered going off the wagon if I don't, you know, REALLY KNOW if it has liquor in it?

Tempted by this possible loophole and a parade of itty-bitty bottles of top-shelf, I flicked open my phone before takeoff and dialed, well, Constance. She was, after all, my sponsor. This was her raison d'être, right?

"McGillicutty's."

I pulled the phone away from my ear.

McGillicutty's?

This wasn't Constance. It was a fellow's voice. And it was a place called...

"McGillicutty's?" I frowned. "Is this 212-555-1894?"

"Yep."

McGillicutty's. Sounds like a goddamned bar.

"Is there a Constance there I could speak with?"

Could you drag her sorry ass out from beneath the bar and revive her for a moment, please?

"Yeah, just a sec."

There was a rustling of cloth. Clothes, maybe. Or...sheets?

"Mmm-hello?"

Her sleepy voice clarified. Sheets.

In some accident of tryptophan and holiday desperation, the woman who had barely left her apartment for two years had something to be thankful for the day after Thanksgiving.

"The guy said this was McGillicutty's." I paused. "This *is* Constance, right?"

"Mmmm-yeah." She yawned. "That's my last name."

Constance McGillicutty was very relaxed, the cob miraculously removed from her ass by not only conversing with someone other than me, but by bedding him. I hadn't the heart to whine.

"I...uh...I just called to see how your holiday was."

"Oh, it was *great*." The man gave a satisfied moan of agreement in the background.

"Yeah, well, okay, then. Bye."

I held my phone, frozen, staring at the passenger nursing her eggnog beside me.

"Huh! Imagine that." I blinked, astonished. "God-damn Constance got laid."

Chapter 22

In New York, it is best to be driven. In California, it is best to drive.

New York offers the happy multi-tasker ample time to make calls, review contracts, apply makeup, change your nylons, et cetera, while waiting in traffic in a chartered car or limousine.

In California, however, there is a satisfying zeal in hitting the open road with your own hands on the wheel. Riding as a passenger on the winding mountain roads lends itself only to motion sickness among even the heartiest of travelers. Being in control and hitting the curves at your own hands, no longer riding bitch or shotgun, but driving...it is exhilarating.

I punched the gas and banked sharply in the rented Benz before turning into the drive through the vined, massive gate of our new home. Water ran down the rocks alongside the walkway, a more natural approach to a fountain. The gardeners had trimmed the lawn, the trees, the flowers. The house itself looked almost polished in the sunlight.

Be it ever so humble.

And on the deck above, crowning the bow of this handsome ship, stood wife and child. Banky waved enthusiastically. Faith sheltered her eyes.

"Hey," I called through the open window, raising my hand.

"Hey." She called back with her own cautious wave.

Twenty-six narrow brick steps up a steep hillside and I was on the deck with them.

Banky latched onto my leg. I ruffled his hair. "Christ!" I panted, smiling. "Where's the service elevator in this joint?"

Banky had resumed the fascinating task of throwing sticks off the deck.

"You got your hair done." She neither smiled nor frowned. "Looks nice."

"Yeah, well, I'm not ready for the dour Gertrude Stein phase, yet. *Tender Buttons,* my ass." I turned to primp at my reflection in the window. "I told him I didn't want it like shoe polish, but to zap all the gray…"

"Now that's the Macy I know." She laughed and caught herself.

I turned. "What?"

"Vain, but charmingly so." She laughed. "Allen called."

Ah, Allen. I'd sold my travel agency to him and his partner, Dave. They and Lavinia were running the show now. Still, they'd booked me on the standard spring lesbian cruise gig. I'd been the hostess for years, and I'd be doing it one last time before passing on the torch. Cozumel in March didn't sound entirely bad. I was actually looking forward to my swan song.

"Am I to call?"

"You are to call." Faith looked up at me. "Macy, I don't know…"

"Shhh." I covered her mouth. "Let's forget about this past week, shall we? Seriously." I wrapped my arms about her. If Faith could forget, so could I. Maybe. "We're on a whole new adventure in our lives together, now. A new place, a new life. It's bound to have rough spots, right?" It sounded scripted, clichéd, a tad insincere, but…it really wasn't.

She nodded up at me.

"Hey, the Brentwood Country Club has a lovely golf course. I drove by on the way in." I put my hands in her hair and gave a playful yank. "Might be a nice place to show our faces."

She gave me a puzzled look. "We don't golf!"

"Sure we do." I smiled. "We're lesbians. Therefore, we golf."

I spun her around and pulled her close to me, my head resting beside hers on her shoulder as we both surveyed the new landscape.

"We'll be all right." I kissed her neck. I'd make the best of this. I'd commit. I'd live here in this beautiful place with my beautiful wife and stick-throwing son. I'd do it because it was right, for all of us. Fuck New York, right?

Right?

"The neighbors have asked us over for dinner, if you're up to it." She squeezed my hand.

Chapter 23

Allen's message disturbed me, not in content, but in tone: *Uh, Macy...we've had some changes for the cruise...give us a call when you can. No rush!*

No rush. There was never a rush of any kind in my life, now. No alarm clock. No real need to distinguish one day from the next, Tuesday from Saturday. I piddled in real estate to keep myself busy, to tell myself I was doing *something*. But the sad truth was, I'd been my own boss, and my boss had retired.

"Look how pretty!" Faith emerged from the bath, toweling her hair. I was doing a slow orbit of the mattress we'd had delivered for the guest room, this mattress being the only bit of furnishing in the house.

"Mah daddy says ah ayum." I shot her a wide smile, batting my eyes, fanning myself with an invisible fan. "And the mayun at the escort agency said yew wanted a purty gurl."

She flicked her towel at me. "Where's the boy?"

"Boy be right here." I pointed through the French doors where Banky sat playing with a one-armed action figure. I'd tried to throw it out and replace it, but apparently he believed in hiring the handicapped, as he'd shrieked until I pulled it from the trash.

Faith took my hand. "He likes it here."

"That he does." I lifted her hand to my mouth and bit it playfully. "So, what are we dealing with tonight?"

The agenda was simple: dinner. As was the location: next door.

"You're a director? For television commercials, did you say?" Without my shoes, I felt somehow demoralized, demoted, and flat-footed. Being shoeless had been a requirement upon entry, however, in the home of Jackie and Janet, the artsy-fartsy lesbotechs next door. It didn't say "take off your goddamned shoes" beneath the huge "J & J" on the door, but it was implied. Heavily.

"Yes. Maybe you're familiar with my work. Have you seen the new spot for Kevin's Heaven?"

My work? Who is this chick? Fellini?

Yes, indeed, I had. Kevin's Heaven was a series of tragically popular angel figurines produced by a lisping, thick-waisted man-boy named Kevin Hartly. Gifted with the "gift of love and sculpture," Mr. Hartly had spewed his collection forth unto the unsuspecting world. Every Coach-toting suburban wifey just *adored* Kevin's Heaven figurines.

I nodded and Faith pinched me, sensing an outburst of honesty.

"Oh, yes!" She stopped pinching me to reply, herself. "Kevin's Heaven! It's everywhere! Great commercial. It's on all the networks."

I threw my head back and flounced. "Kehhhvin's Heahhhven…" Had I had some wine in me, I would have continued the jingle. As it was, I'd performed enough to elicit applause by J & J.

Amazing, these people.

The all-white décor was starting to get to me, not to mention their all-white caftans. I yearned for a dog to enter with sloppy paws or a random earthquake to shatter the fishbowl and spill its contents onto the pristine white rug. No dice.

"There's a real sense of...spiritual magic...surrounding his work." Jackie...or was it Janet?...spoke in elliptical pauses. "He is...a marvelous...man."

Like a 1960s William Shatner in a woman's body.

I smiled at Faith, my eyes narrowed. "I think...we should be...heading back...don't you?"

I'd had enough. Banky had curled up beside me on his mat an hour before. Faith seemed to be shifting about on hers. I was convinced that if we didn't leave shortly, I'd be permanently fused to mine. As their lovely home was so, well, sparse, I had initially assumed that they, like us, were in the process of moving in. This was not so. See, in a minimalist household, one does not have furniture to sit on. One has mats. One also, more than likely, has irreversible hemorrhoids and/or hip dislocation.

"Gosh, yes! We should be going, shouldn't we?" Faith bounced to her feet and helped me to mine. "This has been so nice."

"We'll be seeing you at the gathering, then?" one of the J's queried. "In Topanga?"

Topanga. Home to Faith's childhood friends, the Drabowitz twins. Another reason I was leery of the move.

"Oh, yes! Yes!" Faith was enthusiastic and eager to get the hell out before I blew up and frightened the flakes. "We'll be there."

I reached out, ever the diplomat, to shake hands with the shorter J. She grasped mine with cotton-covered digits. How had this detail of their weirdness slipped by me?

"Pardon my asking, but…" I studied her Mickey Mouse hand. "Why the white gloves? To complete the look?"

"Oh, no…no…" she pooh-poohed. "We're no slaves to fashion."

"We're just a little germ phobic." The other J smiled.

Knock, knock. Who's there? Irresistible opportunity.

Hands locked in front of me demurely, I posed. "I don't know if Faith told you or not, but…I'm not very…close…to most people." I paused for theatrical effect. "I have a lot of walls up, you know? There…now I've said it." I choked back a sob.

This very special CBS movie of the week brought to you by…

The J's nodded sympathetically. Faith tugged at my sleeve. I gave her the "uh-uh" look.

I wasn't quite finished, thank you. I'd survived an evening of tofu, sprouts, and humorless conversation. I had to leave my mark.

"It's just that…" I dabbed at imaginary tears with the back of my fist. "I really need to…open up to people. To share. To…"

I leapt forward, grabbing the smallest J and squeezed the stuffing out of her. I ended the embrace by taking her face in my hands and smooching her right on the tight little lips. She immediately recoiled. I concentrated and let loose with the deepest, wettest cough I could muster, which was, not to brag, pretty impressive, even for an ex-smoker. "Ugh!" I patted my chest. "I just can't seem to shake this. They thought it might be the bird flu, but...oh well, come here, you!"

I reached for the other J and she stepped back. Way back.

"Well, we'll be going, now," Faith said flatly, yanking me by the arm, Banky draped and sleeping over her shoulder.

I blew kisses and hacked as we let ourselves out.

Chapter 24

"You're replacing me with *Jenny Cock*?" My voice echoed. "She looks like a goddamned donkey and you replaced ME with HER?"

Jenny Cock, civilian name Jenny Cochran, was a proud protester, vee-jay, harpist and self-imposed public GLBT spokesperson. Her late-night MTV show, *Rock with Cock* (how clever), had been a cult hit, spawning a coffee-table book along with a string of speaking appearances. She shilled everything on her website from oil filters to coasters bearing her image. She did, indeed, look like the braying mule from *Hee Haw* when she laughed. Now, she was stealing my gig.

"Honey, no one could replace you," Allen schmoozed. "But they want to do a reality show on the boat and they've offered us a shitload of money..."

So that's how it was. Employ someone for how many years, sell them the business at a substantial discount, and they pull this shit on you. All for a few bucks.

Super.

Like Marie Antoinette, I vowed to hold my head high on the way to the guillotine...

"No problem. I'm terribly busy, anyway."

...before I lost my head.

Allen said his goodbyes and hung up.

"Fuck! Fuck, fuck, fuck!" I didn't bother closing my mobile before launching it through one my many kitchen windows.

If I'd stayed in New York I would have never lost my last cruise! My big finale! My last hurrah! Goddamn Jenny Cock with her butch haircut and her out-dated Doc Martens! Goddamn Jenny Cock with her fucking folk guitar!

"What's going on in here?" Faith came in the side door with Banky in tow. She was holding my phone, treading carefully and suspiciously. "We saw this sail out into the garden and thought you might want it back."

What now? Tell her? Let her know that I feel like some pitiful, dried-up old never-was-been? Let the kid see me pull a full-tilt Mommie Dearest flip-out right before his eyes?

"It shocked me. The phone. I mean, they tell you not to use them at the gas pumps, but...Hey!" I brushed the hair out of my face. "Who wants Chinese?"

Chapter 25

They say one of the warning signs of alcoholism is mysterious injuries.

Faith lifted the bag of ice on my ankle. I screamed.

"How'd you do this, again?"

"I fell. After getting the Chinese takeout." *Foot first. Into a dumpster behind Whole Foods. Twelve times.*

"Same ankle as last time?"

I nodded, lifting the steak on my eye to inspect my blue, swollen foot.

Nice to know that cursing and kicking the shit out of a refuse bin in L.A. attracts about as much attention as it would have in New York: none.

Faith clucked her tongue. "Those who don't learn from their mistakes are doomed to repeat them."

"Well, aren't you the little soothsayer this morning."

She shrugged, unpacking a box of dishes. "I'm just saying…"

Banky brought me a box of Kleenex, his standard offering when I was lying prone on my recliner for whatever affliction. I thanked him and patted his head.

"You okay, Mom?"

"Yep." I swung him up onto my lap. "You know how much I love you?"

He smiled and shook his head.

I kissed his left cheek. "More than candy." I kissed his right cheek. "More than shoes."

He laughed. "More than youuuuu?"

He said it to be silly, to make a rhyme, but I looked him square in the eye.

"Oh, yes." I straightened the collar of his shirt. "Much more than me."

Chapter 26

Our front steps, normally a tad precarious, were down-right treacherous to navigate with a bruised ankle. I reached for the driver's-side door handle, and Faith grabbed the back of my jacket.

"Wait a minute there, pal." She pulled my sunglasses down on the bridge of my nose. "How many Percocets have you taken?"

I raised my eyebrows. "None."

She scoped out my pupils closely. "Let me rephrase that: How many *pills*?"

Shit. "One." She gave me the "bullshit" look. "Two." *Shit!* "Okay, three. But I'm a big woman, honey. And they were just Tylenol with codeine."

"Give me the keys."

As the Hummer had not yet arrived from New York, we still had the Benz. And, as with most rentals, it had its quirks.

"Oh, no, no, no. This is not going to work." I was eating my knees. "This seat is stuck. It won't go back."

Faith shifted into gear. "Tough."

Topanga Canyon in the 1960s and 1970s was home

to a number of rock-star hideouts, nudist colonies, and communes. Roads are cut so close to the mountains that you feel bullied. Nature still rules here, with roadside hippies selling rocks and candles, eking out a living and respecting the environment so much it could make you yearn to litter, pillage, and pollute. If there are rock stars still dwelling Topanga, you'd never know it. Either they've all died off or moved to more opulent abodes, trading the privacy of the canyon for the polo ponies of Bel Air.

"I think we should go back." I was actually shaking.

Faith turned off the engine. "Why?"

"I don't know about that girl."

"Delaina? The one we left Banky with?" She touched my hand. "Macy. Settle down. The day care right up the street from our house recommended her. She's worked for them part-time for over a year. I would think they'd know if she were a serial killer."

"What sort of a person sustains themselves working part-time at a day care?" I clutched her hand, wild-eyed. "A drug dealer?"

"The kind of person who lives with her parents and is going to art school."

I put my head down. "Oh."

"Come on." She patted my shoulder. "They said this was going to be a nice party."

"They who? The Edgar Winter sisters?"

Ah, yes. The Drabowitz sisters.

Albino identical twins, they each wore bright white pageboys and pearl earrings to "celebrate their whiteness." Only in Topanga could not one but two albino lesbian sisters survive in the wild. An initial curiosity, I was no longer amused. I'd paid my twenty five cents to see the two-headed calf, thank you. I'd seen enough.

"They creep me out." I shivered. "It's like those twins in *The Shining*..."

Faith rolled her eyes. "Macy..."

I changed my voice to that of a demented British child. "'Come play with us, Danny'..."

"I'd appreciate it if you didn't insult my friends." Faith was getting miffed. "I've known them since I was six."

"Well, I'm sorry. When I can see someone's veins beneath their facial skin...yeesh!" I shuddered. "Besides, they're a bad influence."

And they were. Sort of. The Drabowitzes were self-proclaimed "guerilla journalists" who pounded the local newspaper with wordy editorials criticizing ineffectual local politicians and the like. They wrote scalding reviews for any marginally entertaining film and/or book in the *Topanga Shopper's Weekly* and had self-published three manuals of civil disobedience for the rural lesbian. The Drabowitzes had built their own A-frame cottage out of "100 percent recycled materials" and made all of their clothing. They bore a continuous frown and bitched about everything, most recently that their idea had been stolen.

"I mean, re-usable sanitary napkins?" I scoffed. "That's just gross."

"Well, they're very thrifty people." Faith sighed. "And they did have the idea first. I saw the drawings. They've got an attorney..."

"What, did they carve him out of organic pine?" I snickered. "What's his name? Woody?"

"We don't have to stay long, okay?" Three steps from the car and she mumbled. "I don't know why you think you're better than everyone else. Or why you dressed like we're going to a Kennedy Center fundraiser."

Take my wife. Please.

"What the hell did you say?"

She planted her feet, fists at her sides. "I said I don't know why you think you're better than everyone else!"

"I don't think I'm better than everyone else." I folded my arms. "I just think I'm better than the Drabowitzes."

"And the neighbors. And the babysitter." Faith threw up her hands. "Jesus Christ, Macy, how cool does someone have to be?" She began counting on her fingers. "The Drabowitz twins both graduated from Harvard. The neighbors probably have as much money as you or more. And the babysitter has perfect references. Maybe they're not the ones with a problem. Maybe *you* are. Ever think of that?"

"Oh, what a great revelation!" I threw my hand to my forehead. "How could I ever have been so wrong? Thank you for showing me the light! I'm such a bastard!"

She kept walking.

"I'll just stay in the car while you're at your little happening! Your little 'love in'!" I called after her. "Don't you worry a goddamned bit about me!"

"Here!" She threw the keys at me. "Knock yourself out!"

My cell phone hadn't been the same since its trip through the kitchen window, but it still managed to function, you just had to squeeze and hold the sides. Sure, the back was now held on with duct tape, but it worked. I reached for the keys and heard a bleeeeeep. Constance.

"Every night..." she began.

...it's the same dream.

I sat back on the hood, faint music swelling up from the wooded valley where Faith had gone.

"Hey, Constance." I held an imaginary cigarette to my lips. "How ya been?"

Chapter 27

In the course of an hour and a half, Constance had shared pretty much every traumatic event in her life: incidents on the playground at grade school, bad college roommates. She was really reaching, detailing her recent somewhat unpleasant experience with a fast-food clerk, when I opted to finally hang up and give in to Faith. Making my way down a rocky embankment, I slid on my ass once or twice and cursed myself for not bringing more codeine along for the party. Between my foot and my mood, it couldn't have hurt.

Upon entering beneath the flower-woven arch, I realized that Faith had been right: I was seriously overdressed. Most of these people weren't wearing shoes, let alone a pair of Helmut Lang slings.

I scanned the scene: Maypole dancing *(could there be ecstasy involved?)*, strolling magicians and minstrels *(hide your pocketbooks)*, and a vast table of potluck entrées and sides.

At least there was a cash bar.

"Rum and Coke minus the rum, please." Elbow on the bar, I held up a fin and surveyed the long leg-hairs.

There must have been a helluva sale on gauze tunics somewhere.

"Oh, hey, it's the honor system, man." A mountain of a woman in a black beret arose from behind the bar. "Self-serve."

"Oh." Seeing that it was dusk, and that no one else was wearing them, I pulled off my sunglasses. "So tell me, big girl, what is this...*soirée* anyway?"

She lit a clove cigarette. "Oh, it's grown-up night at the old-fashioned free fair. Mostly for women."

Huh? "Grown-up night?"

"It's the last night, and there's nothing left for kids, anyway. The petting zoo left after PETA made a stink and the puppet show just totally lost its motivation." She sipped from a biodegradable cup. "So what are you, a cop, or somebody's mom?"

"Just a square, Daddio."

"Huh?"

I didn't answer the slack-jawed mountain girl. I would not succumb. I would not wear unbleached muslin or sandals. I would continue to shave my legs and armpits. I was not one of thym, the womyn.

When she finally caught the drift and left, I stepped behind the bar, put my five in the can, and took a Coke. Ice would have been too much to ask, I suppose.

"Hey there, slim." A slightly bow-legged butch in a vest sidled up alongside me. "Buy you a drink?"

What is it with lesbians and vests?

"Thanks, but I just bought one." I raised my plastic glass. "Steer clear of the Coke. It's a tad warm. I think they drink it lukewarm in Mexico, but, well, we're not in Mexico, now, are we?"

"Coke?" She patted my shoulder and rested her hand there. "How about a real drink?"

"I'd love a real drink. I'd love five or six. But I'm a drunk." I stared ahead coolly, flicking at her fingers with my free hand. "And I'm also married. So scram."

I preferred "drunk" to "alcoholic." Sounds much more…retro.

"Okay, okay…" She recoiled. "Goddamn, you see that little number over there?"

Faith? "She's a little out of your league, don't you think, cowboy?"

"What's so bad about me?" She frowned. "I got my own business."

I popped a crab puff I'd swiped from the buffet and chewed. "Cleaning carpets or pet-sitting?"

"What's it to you?" She looked away, nervous. "I bring home plenty of jack, sister."

"That girl is accustomed to blowing more 'jack' in a month than you'll save in a lifetime. You couldn't afford her shampoo bill." I snickered, still chewing. "Good luck."

Life without the buffer of booze had left me rather coarse. After all, I suppose I should have been flattered. Sort of. And as for her cruising Faith and my comments thereafter, for that I felt a little guilty. Maybe a *lot* guilty. Faith had loved me when I was sick and lost when we'd met. She'd loved me because I was kind, or so she thought. My financial status was just gravy on the potatoes.

I found a cocktail napkin and spit out the crab puff.

Frozen at the center. Nice. Slushy crab puffs, warm Coke.

I shook the pleat straight in my slacks.

Note to self: Find decent local dry cleaner. Or a housekeeper that irons.

"Hey, baby..." Faith slurred, giggling and grabbing my ass. "Wanna dance?"

"Whoa!" I jumped, holding her by the shoulders. "Had a couple, have we?"

It wasn't like Faith to drink and certainly not to get soused.

Which one of these gypsy bitches liquored up my wife?

"Yeah." She swayed like a palm tree in the breeze. A petite palm tree that reeked of booze. "And?"

"And nothing." *Shit. Who am I to judge her? I ENVY her.* "Have you had anything to eat?" I took her by the elbow. "Come on, let's get you something..."

"No, no, nooooooo." She sang the words, yanking her arm from my grasp. "Hey!" She poked me in the chest...hard. "Who was that girl who you were talking to?"

"Which one?" I laughed. "Giant beatnik girl or the butch in the vest?"

"Her!" Faith spit as she yelled. "She's the one who brought me the sangria."

"Some schlub offering to buy me a drink." I smoothed her hair. "She also had the gall to comment on you."

"Oh?"

"Mmm-hmm." I smiled. "I told her I didn't think you'd be interested." I kissed her ear, snickering and whispering. "I told her she couldn't even afford your shampoo bill."

"What?!"

"Well, honey, I mean...please." I laughed. "She cleans carpets!"

"You told her that? You actually said that to her?" She was aghast. This was truly an occasion to use that word: aghast. Such occasions are, thankfully, a rarity. "You told her she couldn't afford to buy my shampoo?"

"Well...yeah." I shifted from foot to foot, hands in my pants pockets. "I mean...she was going to hit on you and everything, so..."

"I can't fucking believe it." She stood before me, face flushed. "I cannot believe that you could say something so...so *cruel* to someone."

"Oh, Jesus Christ. I didn't mean it to be cruel. I only meant that, well, you've grown accustomed to a certain lifestyle..."

"Well, at least she finds me attractive!"

Do I come clean about the menopause thing? Do I tell her, now, that it's not just sexual dysfunction, that it's not her fault, that it's because I'm old, father William, and I'm afraid of taking hormones?

Uh...no.

A bigger person would have spilled instead of saying: "Well, if you value her opinion so goddamned much, why don't you go hook up with your little carpet cleaner and get your own little carpet cleaned?"

Her face flushed. "That's right! Why don't I?!" She turned and stomped away.

Oh, shit. "You're forgetting I have the keys!"

"Keep them!" Her voice disappeared into the crowd. "I'll find my *own* way home!"

"Faith!" I called after her angrily, then desperately. "Faith! Wait!"

Nothing.

In the distance, I could see her approaching the vest-wearing, sangria-serving, carpet-cleaning dyke.

I closed my eyes. I saw red.

I took two steps before a good, solid, reasonable thought came to me: *This is not my domain. This is not my crowd. Sure, they may seem like harmless hippies, but they outnumber me and probably wouldn't give peace a chance if I started a scuffle. Pull a punch with Butch and I'm liable to wake up in a ditch with a Buddha figure jammed into my mouth and a crystal shoved up my ass.*

I glanced down at my watch.

Chapter 28

Bang bang Maxwell's silver hammer came down upon her head.

I studied the tip of my cigarette.

Bang bang Maxwell's silver hammer made sure that she was dead…Ba-dump-bump-bump.

Banky had taken a real liking to the Beatles, his favorite CD being *Abbey Road*. I'd played it for him, a few selections, before bed. Now pieces of it floated in my head as I sat on the steps.

I checked my watch: five a.m. Still no wife.

I rang her cell, again. No answer.

The battery's probably run down.

I took a drag and felt my chest harden. I'd missed that in the mornings since quitting.

Ahhhhhhh…

From my perch on the deck stairs, I could see Banky peacefully asleep in his bed. Suddenly, I became quite aware that I was surrounded by quiet, that strange, sleepy California kind of quiet I hadn't yet become used to. This was the sort of place where you could sleep in without being roused by the garbage trucks, if you chose.

Anger? Confusion? Panic? Whatever it was, it chased away the peace and brought back thoughts of the immediate situation at hand.

What if she'd spent the night with that woman?

What if she was missing?

I took another deep drag.

Her family hates me. I might as well dye my hair blonde and head for Mexico like that Scott Peterson asshole, only I'd be innocent, and who really wants to see a pitiful old dyke go to prison?

I imagined a room full of Bible-thumpers raising their hands: We do!

I shook my head. What was I thinking?

Somewhere through the foliage, I heard a sputtering exhaust. Either a crummy motorcycle or some bizarre entry in a lesbian soapbox derby.

A voice gave a hasty goodbye. *Faith.*

Fuck!

I immediately scurried to ditch my cigarette, and then calmed myself.

I'm not twelve. This is America. I can smoke and drink and fuck around and gamble and whatever else I care to do. Besides, I'm not the one out all night with someone who rides a glorified lawnmower.

The gate hummed open. She came slinking up the steps, watching her feet as she came.

I stretched and crossed my legs at the ankle. "Good morning."

"Oh!" Faith jumped. "Oh my God, you scared me!"

"I don't see why." Said the spider to the fly. One cigarette and my voice was already deeper, more sinister.

She gave a little laugh. I stared at her, stoic.

"Well, this is something." I sat up. "I don't think I've ever seen you with a hangover. Maybe I should take a Polaroid."

"I'd fill a baseball stadium if I had a photo for every time I saw you with a hangover."

"*Touché.*" I blew out a stream of smoke. "I called you six times."

She advanced a step. "Can I get past you, please?"

I stubbed out my cigarette, holding my position on the steps. "Not just yet."

Faith sighed heavily. "What do you want, Macy?"

"What do I want?" I glowered down at her, the angry green giant. "I'll tell you what I want. I want to know where you spent the night last night."

I gave her a head to toe inspection. Unlaced shoes. Crumpled pants. Blouse buttoned wrong.

Is that strange perfume I smell, or strange pussy?

Faith clenched her jaw. "At a friend's."

I felt a twinge beneath my sternum.

Super. One cigarette and I'm going to have a fucking heart attack. That's just great. Who knew karma could work so fast?

I sat back down.

Don't grab your chest, asshole, or you'll be tipping your hand. Don't let her see you're weak. You are the angry green giant. You are King Kong...

"Oh..."

...as he tumbles down from the Empire State Building.

"...shit."

"Macy?"

I felt the brick steps hit my shoulder blades. I tore

105

the buttons off the center of my blouse, clutching my chest. This wasn't a heart attack. This was asthma. Panic asthma. Again.

I think.

California may have brought a better climate and better air, but it couldn't stop how adrenaline often rapidly closed my airways.

"I can't get my breath..." Ah, the choppy, hurried speech. Here it was, the old fish out of water routine. Faith stepped over me and ran up to the house, leaving me to flop and gasp on the steps.

Don't leave me! I have so much to offer! Please! I have a gold card! I have real estate! I have the magic tongue!

"It's okay." Faith knelt and cradled my head, holding the inhaler to my lips. "It's okay."

And in a few minutes, it *was* okay. Aside from the normal shakes from the medication, I felt fairly fine. But how she looked at me...it wasn't the warm smile I was accustomed to.

"Baby." My voice cracked. "Tell me you didn't sleep with the degenerate you spent the night with. Tell me that, please." I shut my eyes hard. "Please."

"I didn't."

She helped me sit up and then sat down beside me. "I passed out on her couch. We're just friends, Macy. She brought me home as soon as I stopped throwing up this morning. Nothing happened."

"You got sick?" I wrinkled my brow, exaggerating my concern.

"Oh, yes." She rubbed the back of her neck. "I got sick, all right."

Serves you right. If you'd stopped sucking down the sangria and left the party with me, you would have been just fine.

Faith clasped her hands around her knees. "Buying this house...it was a mistake."

Whew. Maybe now we can go back home. New York: filthy and fantastic.

Home sweat home.

I tried to hide my euphoria. "You think so?"

She nodded. "I'm sorry, but I just don't think this is going to work."

"Me, either." I put my arm around her and felt her stiffen.

"I'm talking about us." She pointed to me, then to herself. "Us."

"Us." I let my arm drop down behind her. I felt faint, deflated. My ears began to ring slightly. "Us. Yes. Of course." I stood and steadied myself against the rail. "Of course."

The sun rose slowly beyond the trees. All was quiet, that California quiet, as Faith slipped into the house behind me and turned on the shower.

Chapter 29

"You're so handsome, it's a crime." I parted Banky's hair on the side, combing the curls back from his forehead. "It is, Banky. It's positively criminal."

"I don't like these shoes." He frowned, kicking at his reflection in the floor. "They don't fit good."

"They fit fine. They're just new." I swatted his butt and stood. "Why don't you go out on the deck and break them in a little?"

I slid open the glass door and Banky stomped ahead of me, still frowning but heading for a toy truck he'd left out earlier. I lit a cigarette.

"Today's going to be just swell." I exhaled, smiling. "Everything's going to be fine. She'll never leave me. I mean, goddamn, I just bought her the house of her dreams! So we've hit a rough patch. Everybody has their rough patches. We're no different than any other couple trying to..."

"Mom?" Banky tugged at my pants leg. "Who are you talking to?"

"Oh, nobody." I smiled. "Just blowing smoke."

"Hey." Faith padded out onto the deck in her robe, nursing a cup of coffee.

"Oh, hey!" I flicked my cigarette. "Have a good nap?"

"Yeah, thanks. Banky?" She opened the door. "Play inside for a few minutes, okay?"

He pushed his truck inside obediently, settling on the floor in front of the sofa, still within our sight.

Faith squeezed my shoulder. "Thanks for making coffee."

"I figured you could use some." I stubbed out my cigarette. "Banky's all set for his play date." I laughed. "He hates those shoes…"

"Macy?"

I fumbled with my lighter, distracted. "Yes?"

"Maybe we just need a break, you know?" Faith rubbed my upper arm and looked out at the horizon. She smiled, pleading her case…or was it out of pity? "Just some time to…you know…re-evaluate things."

"Look, I need to run into town, anyway." I felt my pocket for my keys. "We're out of paper towels and I…"

"Six months." Obviously she'd given this some thought. The hangover haze had lifted. "I think that would give us enough time to decide what direction we need to move in."

She sounded so formal, so grounded, that I almost believed her. Almost.

I broke loose of the numbness and looked her in the eye.

"What about the boy?" I said. "When will I be having Banky?"

"Well, I-I don't know." Faith stammered. "I hadn't really thought about…"

"Well you damned well better think about it!" I felt my neck flush with anger.

Faith leaned in. "Keep your voice down."

"You are not going to keep me from seeing my boy," I hissed. "Do you understand that?"

"Macy, you are getting way out of control over this." Faith stepped back. "I never said you couldn't see him."

Oh, but I'd seen this coming. I'd seen it coming when she'd come straggling home. I just hadn't wanted to believe it. I couldn't believe that I was about to lose my wife and son in 100 spoken words or less. Bang. Over. Adiós. History.

"Six months, Mace." She softened her tone. "That's all I'm asking. We'll work something out about Banky. It's just a little time to reassess things, okay?" She paused, clapping me gently on the shoulder. "Okay?"

I nodded, averting my eyes before they spilled.

"Macy..."

"I'll be back in a few." I pushed past her gently and headed down the steps.

In the Mercedes, a mile or so past our home, the dam broke. I pulled to the side of the road, slamming my fists on the dash.

My father, Wild Bill Delongchamp, was a looker. Women looked at him, men looked at him, children were drawn to him instantly. Descended from assorted French peasants, lowlifes, and even the Marquis de Sade (or so it was rumored), my father, nonetheless, looked like a king on a postmodern chess board. And Vi had been his queen.

I was fourteen-years-old the day I saw him standing, hands jammed into his pants pockets, staring out at the still, glistening water of our backyard swimming pool. Dad swam every day, he was strong and long and lean, so it was odd that he skipped his laps this particular morning. Instead, he stood. Thinking, I suppose. Thinking, his hair parted neatly on the side, his usually tousled bangs slicked back, shirt collar open.

I blinked from the sun as it caught the crystal of his watch. I noticed he was tapping his foot. And I had this sense that this moment of poolside contemplation was the prelude to...something.

"Bill!" It was a gregarious greeting, a big, hairy, back-slapping greeting from Nickie Love, Piqua's area wise guy. Beside him, my father looked even more polished and civilized. Beside my father, Big Nickie looked like a knuckle-dragging ape.

Nickie began talking about baseball, and though I had my reasons for being angry with him, his manner of telling a story was undeniably seductive. His arms gestured wildly, his eyes flashed, he laughed long and loud. He had my attention, and he usually had Dad's.

But this time, no dice.

Dad's posture didn't change, didn't relax, and I had my suspicions of why lightning was about to strike. Suddenly he turned on his heel to face Nickie and said, "I know you're fucking my wife."

Unlike most conflicts, this was one I didn't want to be a secret spectator for. I was afraid, not just that Nickie might pull a weapon or use his meaty hands to make waste of my father, but because of this new father I was seeing for the first time.

"You cocksucker, I know you're sleeping with Vi."

He'd never hit me, never been violent with anyone as far as I knew, but my father lunged for Nickie Love, knocking him into the pool and leaping in after him.

Obviously, what was good for the gander was NOT good for the goose.

"Dad!"

My scream bounced on the glass of the window. I opened it and screamed again.

"Dad!"

They were thrashing about, and at last I saw my father's arm around Nickie's neck from behind, forcing him beneath the water.

My screams had rousted our housekeeper from the laundry room. She ran blathering in Spanish toward the pool and at last my father let go, backing away from Nickie, pulling himself up the steps.

"Dad?" I held the door, still not sure if I wanted to stay inside or venture into this scene. "Dad?" He was soaked, blood streaming from his nose, hair hanging in his eyes, suit jacket ripped.

"You go inside, Marcella," he said, slogging over the pavement to loom over Nickie Love as he cowered and choked.

I watched him extend a hand and help Nickie to his feet and point him to his car.

"Go on inside, Marcella." He sat down, dangling his shoes in the water, his head in his hands. "Go on inside."

And for nearly an hour, I watched my father cry.

Chapter 30

They say your first real love is your mother. I tend to agree.

I sat on the hood of the car and chain-smoked for a good hour at the side of the road.

I drew back my foot and banged it against the grill.

Here it was, a memory I didn't want, but had retrieved after the log jam had busted loose in my psyche.

"Mom, can I lick the bowl?"

Like I needed to ask.

My mom was a great cook. Her cakes were legendary at the annual Piqua Pig Roast and Bake Sale. As but a mere squirt, I hovered about the kitchen habitually hoping to score some of her cast-asides, and it was me, not Elliott or Dad, that always got to run my fingers around the edges of her mixing bowl and taste that red velvet cake batter.

Vi hadn't read books to me, as she assumed what seemed like another male role (if stereotypical) in the household: come home from work, have dinner, retire to her chair beside the fire, get casually bombed sipping whiskey and smoking cigarettes as she read the newspaper and talked. We'd been inseparable, Vi and I, and I'd felt safer with her than with anyone, but she had surpassed the obvious housewife identity and entered into a decidedly businessman arena. This had been the role I'd predicted for myself upon hearing of Faith's pregnancy with Banky. You know: return home from closing a contract in my post-retirement real estate career, collapse in my chair with pipe and slippers at hand, ruffle the boy's hair, and ask Beaver, "How was school?"

This, however, wasn't what I'd become.

I'd become…a mommy.

I was the one who read books to Banky. I was the one who hauled out the video footage of his birth on the evening of his first birthday. I bathed him and snuggled him and loved him so much it scared me. He'd been the clincher in my decision to quit drinking and smoking and acting like a rat packer. I was the one he came screaming to after nightmares, sleeping the rest of the night on my chest, his arms wrapped about me for the warmth and love necessary to survive his dreams.

Goddamn her.

You see flaws in your parents that you hate in yourself.

Goddamn her.

Maybe remembering Mom's problems with Valium, hostility, and emotional weakness only reminded me of my own shit, you know? Maybe I'd been too hard on her, hating her for my own problems more than hers, not seeing that she'd passed along good traits as well as bad. I did, after all, always let Banky lick the bowl.

Goddamn her.

Faith would steal this from me?

Snapshots of our relationship flashed before me.

Laughing. Camping. Assembling a bookcase. Making love.

How could she throw this all away?

Goddamn her.

Shock can leave gaps in your reality. Shock can make your mind skip little sequences, take you in and out of the game, leave you awakening from trauma as if part of your memory has been erased. You know you drove to your destination, but you don't remember how you got there. You know your hair is damp, but you don't recall taking a shower. It's unsettling to say the least, knowing you're one little pill away from having a nervous breakdown. One step further and you're just a chart in some doctor's hand at the mental facility.

"Trish." Even in my shaken state, I remembered her number. I felt confident at first, excited, even, to re-tie our ties together and make nice over the phone. But when she answered, the bottom fell out of my resolve. I didn't know why I'd called. Maybe I didn't want to know.

"Hello, Macy."

So what do you say to someone who'd kicked you out of her life indefinitely?

"I'm sorry."

Car accidents. Gunshot wounds. Why do people often apologize when they're the victims themselves?

"Macy?" She sounded concerned.

"I love you." I sniffled, shading my eyes from the sun. "I just wanted to tell you that."

One push of a button and I ended the chance of conversing any further. Indefinitely.

I'd run out of my Cymbalta prescription over the weekend. Cymbalta had been my lifesaver after quitting the sauce, helping to even out the moods and shake the sinking despair that overtook me at inopportune times (I cried in the organic fruit section of Whole Foods, in the changing rooms of Neiman Marcus, in cabs and hotel lobbies, during re-runs of *Dallas*). Gripping the wheel of the Benz, not knowing how or why I'd ended up at the parking area of the Reel Inn on Pacific Coast Highway, I began to realize I needed to get it refilled…soon. It's a sad realization that you can't just get a grip on your own, that your own biology is betraying you.

"Comfortably Numb" came on the radio. I laughed. If there was a God, he or she had a helluva sense of humor.

Hellloooo…is there anybody in there…?

Staring across the Pacific Coast Highway, I saw the ocean slamming itself against the rocks. It was spitting rain now, too much for anyone but a handful of tourists to be beachcombing. No lifeguards or surfers. No swift-swimming locals to save the day. Eyeing the bent guard rail, it hit me, then, that this was my chance, the best chance I had at giving in and giving out.

I leaned into the wind, arms spread, a hood ornament in linen slacks. Cars whipped past as I leisurely crossed the highway.

Goddamn her and the whole fucking world.
Goddamn Cymbalta.

I paused at the top of the cliff. It would be quite a trek or tumble down the scrubby hillside before I reached the shore. Still, the promise of the frothy, waiting waves seduced me. I imagined a bubbling demise, my life flashing before me in an ultra-cinematic fashion, complete with soundtrack (anything but "Candle in the Wind"): Taking my first steps, riding a bicycle, the first feel of another woman's boob in my hand, my first hit of ecstasy. Beautiful, beautiful moments.

Oh, the drama of it all. The unholy dyke drama of it all.

My mind flipped through the pages of Hollywood Babylon, settled itself on the Lupe Velez chapter. Poor Lupe, Tarzan's jilted lover, knocked up and unable to face the ridicule and rejection. Poor Lupe, who took her own life by taking too many pills and then drowning in the toilet as she upchucked burritos and barbiturates.

Oh, senorita, you were living in Hollywood, so close to the ocean. Why didn't you plunge into the surf and flush yourself down the biggest toilet of them all?

But as soon as the film of my last seaside journey came to mind, as soon as I saw myself suck in the blue and sink like the battered old barge that I was, I stopped. The film ended. The drama was over. *Fin.* Faith would move on. Banky would forget his other mommy. The world would continue on without me.

This pissed me off, righteously.

Hadn't I worked all of my life to leave some sort of mark, some evidence of my existence?

I let my arms fall to my sides. I hadn't accomplished anything of any real importance yet. No serious philanthropic efforts, no cure for herpes. My passing on would pass on nothing to the world, save for my spot in the parking garage and some fantastic real estate being up for grabs.

I stood straight and tall, hands on my hips. I wasn't ready to wash the life out of myself just yet. Sure, cold water is a fine preservative, but even at fifty-two my bod was too good to sacrifice to the fishies.

Inside the Reel Inn, I took a seat at a booth. An ant leisurely crawled across the red and white plastic table-cloth. I watched its delicate legs move it along, reminding myself that those legs weren't delicate at all: An ant can carry several times its own weight, according to some *National Geographic* shit I'd read in a doctor's waiting room.

I let the ant continue until it disappeared into a crack on the wood-paneled wall. No squishing. Far be it for me to hinder the progress of something so little and so strong.

I stuck a cigarette between my lips and let it dangle as I struck match after match, or rather, attempted to strike them. My hands weren't quick or steady enough to make a flame. I cursed myself for having thrown out my old reliable Zippo and dried my eyes.

"Can't smoke here anyhow," a twangy, rather mush-mouthed voice came from above. I looked up to find a lanky redhead far past her prime wearing jeans, a Bud-weiser t-shirt, and sensible shoes. Apparently I'd discovered the modern-day Flo. She pulled a Bic out of her pocket and flicked a flame.

"Ah, hell, there's nobody here, anyhow."

I took a drag. Normally, I'd be a little suspicious of her good nature. However, I was in no mood to give a shit. "Thank you." It sounded formal and stiff, a timid smile accompanying the phrase. "That's very kind of you."

"Oh, no problem. I'll bring you an ashtray. Just flick it on the floor, for now." She pulled a pad of paper from her back pocket, a pen from the pile of hair on her head. "So, what'll you have, sugar?"

I cleared my throat. "I...um..." I sat up. "Do you, perchance, offer O'Leary's?"

Ah, yes, O'Leary's: the near beer I'd learned to fall back on when my soul demanded at least the vague taste of alcohol.

"Oh, sure." She scribbled on the pad. "Care to partake in any of our succulent specials of the day?" She smirked, and I'm still not sure if she was cracking wise at my formality or just being silly.

"Just an O'Leary's, please."

She cocked her head and looked squarely into my eyes. "You all right, hon?"

"I'm fine." I took another drag, my cig hand trembling visibly.

Jesus Christ on a bike...

"Oh, yeah, you're just peachy." She touched my hand with hers to steady it, a hand with long fingers and painted nails much like mine. "Come on, now. A big rawboned gal like yourself, you need to have something to eat."

I was in no state to accept folksy wisdom. "Really. I'm not..."

"I'll bring you some oysters. You look like the type." Flo spun around and made for the kitchen. Out of habit, I watched her ass, which wasn't that bad. She returned almost as quickly as she left and slapped an ashtray on the table, sitting down across from me. "You know, I used to smoke. I quit that shit years ago, though. Switched to these."

Flo let what looked to be a tiny pack of heroin flick out between her upper and lower teeth, sucking it back in like a snake with its tongue.

I spoke before thinking. "What the fuck is that?"

She threw her head back and laughed. "Tobacco." She leaned in, sharing the secret. "They put it in these little pouches so it doesn't get messy."

"Chewing tobacco?"

"Yeah, but it's not nasty like that." She nodded out the window. "I saw your little display out there."

I composed a confused look but felt myself blushing. Had I been so obviously desolate that an aging waitress in a place advertising "fish tacos" could see my soul so easily?

"Honey, if you think you're the first to contemplate suicide overlooking the ocean, you're very much mistaken." She looked out the window, her eyes softening. "Saw a feller take all of his clothes off and walk right into traffic in that spot over there." She sighed. "It's a hard life, I guess. I don't know why people come to the ocean so much to bump themselves off, but they do."

"They say most of the human body is water," I said, relaxing a bit and following her gaze to a guardrail. "Maybe that has something to do with it."

"Maybe." Still looking at PCH, she casually snatched my hand as I lifted it to smoke. "Let's put this out." She took my cigarette and stubbed out its glowing end in the tin ashtray.

I laughed. "Why? Is it bothering you?" *I mean, you're the one who gave me a light.*

"No, but it's bothering *you*." She sat back and raised an eyebrow. "Looks like you're still trying to kill yourself one way or another, aren't you, slick?"

I nodded, conceding. I felt a little better then. It was nice to have someone care, even a stranger. You get what you get, and at that point I wasn't getting much.

Show me the love, Big Red.

She frowned, turning her back and walking away from me.

"Go on," she said. "Go on home and get some rest. It'll all look better tomorrow."

I stood. "I can't go home."

She spun around, peeved but not really peeved. "Then go to a nice hotel. Take a good long bath. Order room service. Treat yourself."

Tears formed in my eyes, ready to flood. "I don't want to be alone."

God, I'm pathetic.

Red turned to the window and huffed. "Weatherman said it'd be clear as crystal today, and look at this bullshit." She shook her head. "I only live about a mile from here. What say you save me from walking home and give me a ride, sailor?"

Was she hitting on me? Would she invite me in for coffee and want something more, and what's more, would I give it to her? Was she just feeling sorry for me? And why did she remind me of my mother?

I said nothing, puzzled but curious and eager for the distraction. I mean, I had nowhere to go. I was a refugee; a woman without a country and, more important, a woman without her wife, child, and cosmetics travel case. Any port in a storm, they say, so I took her home.

Home was a silver trailer shaped like a Monistat suppository. It glistened in the rain, obviously painstakingly waxed and polished. Red led me up the steps and the interior was just as I'd thought: immaculate. Simple people take care of their things, I thought and nodded to myself, vowing to learn something from this and perhaps study the ways of more primitive folk. Simple people appreciate what they have. Not that Red was a Quaker, but things were clean and uncluttered. A small Chinese carpet lay before the television, and bookshelves were organized by last name, from Capote to Whitman.

"Nice place you have here." I said. The furnishings were tasteful, even chic. I put on my glasses and studied a print hanging above the sofa.

"Hey! This is a Chamberlain!" I arched my brows in disbelief, moving in to study the signature. "Yes, it sure as hell is!"

"Oh, that?" Red called out from the kitchen. "Yeah, I picked that up at one of her shows last fall. It's only a print, but…"

"Which show? The one on Second Street?"

"I think so."

"I was there!" I spun around. "I was there, too! Huh! Well, isn't that something!"

"Yes, that is." Red came into the living area carrying two cups. "Coffee? It's decaf. Didn't think I should give you the real stuff."

"Thank you!" I still couldn't believe it. It wasn't my mother she reminded me of. It was me. Me, if I'd waited tables in some shit-kicker bar. Me, if I had a lot less money and a lot more common sense.

Red and I sat and talked and laughed much of the night about art and people she'd met in her travels.

"I helped build an orphanage in Romania a few years back." She produced photos of her looking dirty and happy alongside other dirty, American, happy people. "Getting there was no fun, but it sure was a good time."

Judging me as "spent and no use to no one" in the shape I was in at around eleven p.m., she insisted I take her bed.

"I mean it," she said. "Go on and get your ass in there and go to sleep."

And I did just that. She had a heated mattress pad and I nearly moaned with comfort. Not a surprise when I fell asleep within minutes. Not a surprise, also, that I had a nightmare. This time, it was snakes. I awoke in the echo of a scream, covered in sweat.

Red peeked in. "You okay?"

"Justabaddream." I was telling myself this as much as her, my asthma kicking in. "Couldyoupleasebring me…mypurse."

She hurried there and back, sitting beside me as I huffed.

"Thank you."

"Don't mention it." She put her arm around my shoulders, then recoiled. "You're soaking wet."

Red made her way to a chest of drawers. "Yeah, this one will about fit."

She handed me a very long, very flannel, very *Little House on the Prairie* nightgown.

"Oh." I smiled, frightened by this frilly monstrosity. "That's...that's okay. I'll be fine."

"Oh, no. No, no." Red moved for the door. "Go on and change. I'll be back in a few minutes to make sure you have." She shooed. "Go on, now."

I unfolded the gown. Ugh. Who knew that there was actually a fabric created with a tiny "pig wearing sunglasses" pattern?

Fearing the wrath of Red, I changed. Moments later, she knocked and emerged with a glass of water in one hand, her other hand closed. She, too, was wearing the famed "pig in sunglasses" nightgown. "Take this."

It was a tiny white crescent. I shook my head.

"No way." Before, I would have leapt at a handful of these babies, whatever they were. Now, I was afraid. "I'm sorry. I can't. I used to abuse drugs."

She seemed interested. "What did you abuse?"

"Nearly everything you can think of except laxatives."

Dropping the pill in a wastebasket, Red crawled over to the other side of the bed and lay there. "Come on up here and take a rest."

"No, that's alright, thanks." Like I was rejecting cream or sugar.

I'm trying to cut down.

"Come on, now." She cocked her head. "I'm not trying to get into your panties. Come on."

So I did. I obeyed. I crawled up beside Big Red and let her pull me against her, my head in her cleavage.

"Shhhh." She held me, letting me rest against her and relax.

And there in the valley of her ample southern titties, I felt safe and warm.

"A big old baby is what you are." I heard her chuckle as I was drifting off. "Just a big old baby."

Chapter 31

Having snuck out of Marlboro Red's trailer at the crack of dawn, I sat peeling back the paper to take bites out of my breakfast in the parking lot of All American Hamburger. Desperation spawns strange bedfellows, as well as strange dietary needs.

Spying myself in the rearview mirror, I nodded.

Yes, you look like hell.

Burger in hand, I hacked and thumped my chest.

Ah, the smoker's cough. Back by popular demand.

I blinked and found myself zooming up Sunset.

This cannot be happening.

I slipped on my sunglasses.

Nobody does this to me.

I clicked off the clamor of the morning radio.

Did I just cut off Richard Simmons? And did the little fucker just flip me off?

Back in the canyon, I lit a cigarette once again and rested my ass against the hood of the Benz, surveying the palm ruins behind the Uplifters Rec Center Park.

I need a drink.

I smirked and felt the sweat collect at the nape of my neck.

See what happens? You start by caving in on the cig-arettes, and now...

Booze. I could see it all in my mind. Vodka, tequila, and gin...oh, my! All lined up in pretty bottles against the bar, backlit and transformed into a multi-colored blur of lights.

Just look! Every day is Christmas at Pete's Tavern! Ho! Ho! Ho!

"Constance! How the hell are you?" I half shouted into the flap of my flip.

Every night she dreams of a head in a Tiffany box. Every night I dream of Cuervo straight up on the rocks. Hey, that rhymes...

"Macy! Blerr...mrlerr." I didn't care what she was saying. I responded out of habit. "Oh, not too much. Just relaxing in the sun out here!"

I punched my lines like I was the new host of *Let's Make a Deal*.

Or, rather, *Let's Make A Drink*.

"So, Constance, you've got a new gentleman friend?"

To anyone else, I may have sounded just swell. But a drunk knows a drunk, and no matter how bubble-headed Constance was, she knew what was up. It's in-stinctive. We're all rotten apples that have fallen from the same tree.

"Macy?"

I took a deep drag. "Yes?"

For once, Constance was listening and calm. "Talk to me."

Chapter 32

A thick cable was affixed to the leaning trunk of the coral tree by the guest house, anchoring it into place. If this place was anything, it was well-tended.

I tapped the tree trunk with the toe of my calfskin Hermès slipper, legs dangling, sunglasses on in the dawn, perched on a thick branch that arched over the walkway to our house.

And the thought of someone lying next to her during this "trial separation," of someone else fucking her, made me boil.

I lit a cigarette. The thought of someone else tossing my boy into the air, giggling with him, and watching him grow up made me boil even more.

Smoke stung my eyes as I pushed off from the branch and let my feet hit the mossy bricks with more grace than I'd expected.

My neck felt hot. I undid another button on my blouse.

What now, Faith? Sit at home with my thumb up my ass and pay for your Pilates lessons?

I huffed. My heart sank in my chest. I felt dizzy, used, betrayed.

Easy, big girl. You just need a shower.

I hugged the tree trunk, steadying myself.

No need for alarm, now. No need to have a hissy.

I took off my shades and rubbed my eyes.

We've been abusing our prescriptions, now, haven't we? Skipping the anti-depressants? Double-dipping the pain killers?

I sighed.

Too much and boom…your heart explodes and she gets everything behind curtain number three without a fight. Says so in your will. One puff of Proventil too many and you're nothing but Casper the fucking ghost, my friend.

"I need a rest," I said aloud to myself. "A couple of days somewhere pleasant."

You don't need a rest, fucko. You need a DRINK.

I nodded. "And how."

So what's stopping us? There's a liquor store up the street. The muse awaits!

I rubbed the back of my neck. "No. No way. Oh, no you don't."

Oh, come ON! Don't tell me we've become one of those California crunchy granola types in this short of time!

Pain pressed from my breastbone through to the center of my back.

"It's all right." I took a deep breath, as deep as I could, anyway. "It's probably just gas."

It's probably the big one, Lizzabeth!

I sat down on a bench and closed my eyes to escape the darkening periphery.

Just one drink and this will all go away. The swimming head, the palpitations, the sweats...all gone if we just find the nearest bar and take the Nestea plunge.

"Shut up!"

And then, a voice from the foliage. "Macy?"

I felt clammy and shaken. I didn't bother to turn my head.

"Yeah."

Faith emerged and stopped short of touching me. "You don't look well."

"Well, pardon me if I'm not rosy-cheeked and perky, love, but what do you expect?" I stood and lit a fresh cig, suddenly quite aware that I looked disheveled, withered, and crazed. "I need a shower," I said, staring at the bricks beneath my feet.

"Um..." She cocked her head, inspecting.

"No, seriously." I managed to smile. "Kindly step aside. I need a shower and some coffee. Desperately."

"Macy, last night..." She put her hands on her hips. "Did you drink last night?"

"Ha!" I raised my arms to the sky. "I WISH!"

"I mean it." She wasn't budging. "Did you?"

"I fucking said I didn't, didn't I?" My voice became deeper, darker, almost male. "Now step aside so I can go upstairs and have a goddamned cup of coffee. Please."

She set her jaw. "I don't think you're in any shape to be around Banky. He's getting acquainted with Delaina right now. I don't think we should disturb them."

"Look." I grinned, my eye twitching. "In case you've forgotten, this is MY fucking house. I'm the one on the deed. So get your little ass out of my way. Mommy needs to put her feet up and have a cappuccino."

"No way." She was afraid, I could tell. And the sick thing was...I *liked* it. "I'm not letting you up there. Not how you are now."

Before I knew it, a patio chair had left my hands and was smashing through the guesthouse sliding door. "You won't *let* me?" I lunged for her and grabbed her by the front of her blouse. "You have ruined me, do you understand that? You've RUINED me! You're taking everything away from me! You're *killing* me!"

She started to cry. I let her go and covered my ears to stop the ringing.

Chapter 33

A nut house is a lot like jail. It doesn't matter if you surrender; the doors are still locked after they close behind you. Along with your belt, your shoelaces, your cigarettes, you also lose your rights. You are now a bitch of the system.

"Look, I just need my meds." I steepled my fingers at the smiling, white-coated tribe sitting across the table. "I'm a recovering alcoholic and I take an anti-depressant. So if you could just fill my 'script, I'll be on my way."

"I don't think so, Mrs. Delongchamp." The doctor had her hair pulled back so tightly that her eyes were slightly slanted. "From our intake questionnaire, I see you haven't been to an AA meeting in weeks..."

"It's MISS Delongchamp." I smiled. "And no, I haven't. I've just moved here and..."

"And you've considered suicide in the last forty-eight hours."

I shrugged. "Well, yeah, but then I met this waitress..."

Doctor Tight-bun folded her arms. "I think you should probably stay with us for a few days." She smiled like the Grinch Who Stole Christmas. "Now let's get you all settled in, okay?"

"Absolutely not!" I cracked my knuckles. "I'm not some wacko off the street! I have rights! I have an attorney!"

"I legally can and will have you physically detained until I get a court order to keep you here, at least overnight."

Thus was my welcome to the Cedars-Sinai Psych Unit.

Strait jacket and tie required.

Chapter 34

"My Macy."

The voice was soft and low and comforting. Husky from whiskey. Strong, yet feminine. Very sultry. Very...Vi?

Oh, God...not another bathroom stall hallucination.

But this time, I wasn't in a bathroom stall, and this time it was Vi. Vi Rogers, my mentor, heroine of my youth, step-motherly fashionista from another era. She was perched on the edge of my bed in her red silk suit, cigarette in one hand, drink in the other.

"How's it going, kid?"

I could have pinched myself, could have screamed or searched my mind for a logical explanation, but I didn't want logic.

I wanted Vi.

I clutched her close, hearing the ice clink in her glass as I rested my head on her shoulder, sobbing. She held me with her free arm, rubbing my back in that circular motion, the way she used to do.

The way Faith used to do, too.

"How's the ticker?"

I pulled back, still absorbing her strong features, slight build, impeccable taste, and presence. I'd missed so many things about Vi that I'd forgotten how many until seeing her again.

"My God, Vi, what am I gonna do?" I covered my face and fell against her, letting her rock me, bawling and choking.

"So your girl isn't the swingin' doll you thought she was, eh, sugar?"

Ah, Vi. Always with that super cool Frank Sinatra method of speech.

"She's turned on me, Vi." I shook my head. "I'm so confused. I don't want to lose her, and I can't bear to lose Banky."

"You mean little Bill?" She laughed. "That one's going to break some hearts."

"I can't lose him, Vi."

She winked and straightened the collar of my gown. "Well, then. You know what you have to do, don't you?"

And I did. Right then, I remembered what she'd done.

Right then, I knew what was necessary.

Chapter 35

Our house was never quiet when we were growing up. Whether it was the afternoon blast of T-Rex albums from Elliott's room or the perpetually perking coffee, there was always a soundtrack of underlying noise that wasn't particularly invasive. It was when the noise stopped that put us all on alert. One such still, solemn period set the scene for a major row between my parents.

They'd been fighting all weekend, Vi and Dad. They were quiet with each other, each one mourning the hopefully temporary loss of good conversation, good camaraderie, good sex. I wasn't particularly afraid of what might happen until Vi entered my room that morning carrying a suitcase.

This time it was about Thanksgiving. While Dad cared to opt for the usual visit to Mom's, sucking down homemade stuffing and unbuttoning his pants afterward to discuss my brother Elliott's latest brush with the law with his ex-wife, Vi put her foot down. She wanted a dinner just for us at a Chinese restaurant.

"You ever have an egg cream, kid?" She pulled open my dresser drawer and began plucking items to pack.

"Boy, it's really something. A real egg cream is about the best thing in the world. And the only place to get them is New York."

Vi punctuated further packing with tales of Macy's Thanksgiving Day Parade, a spectacle I'd witnessed most every one of my eight years on the tube.

And now, well, I was going to see it live and in person.

We left while Dad was at work. Vi had called in sick...I'd heard her...and within just a few hours I had my first glimpse of New York City. Popping over a hill and heading for a toll booth, a great, gray Oz appeared through the windshield of our taxi cab.

"What do you think, kid?" Vi had fortified herself on the plane with numerous baby bottles of bourbon. She slurred a little, and for the first time it made me nervous. "Tomorrow's the big parade. It's something you'll never forget, I promise."

She seemed a little crazy, a little off-kilter. Vi at her drunkest had never seemed out of control, but on this day she was laughing nervously and holding back tears. I was eight, and confused. I was afraid of this place, this dirty backdrop of a city, and though I smiled and nodded as she pointed out various attractions, all I wanted was to cover her up with a blanket on the plane and let her pass out on the way back to Piqua.

We stayed in decent digs. The Plaza: an impressive palace even to a kid, if a little intimidating. From what I'd seen on television, it looked like a fortress where the Pope would live, all garish and gold. I held Vi's hand on the elevator tightly. I knew that if we were separated, both of us would be screwed.

"I'm not coming home, Bill." I heard her talking in the other room of our suite. "Tell her she can have you back. I don't care anymore."

The "she" in question was, I presumed, Mom. And Vi did care. Though Dad had trimmed back his time spent as Mr. Fix-It at Mom's, he still carried a torch for his first love and didn't have the balls to move on from her completely. Vi knew this. The whole fucking world knew this. And it ate at Vi well into the night, leaving her staring into the flames of our fireplace at least a couple of times a week.

While I couldn't think of anyone I'd rather be kidnapped by, I still felt uncertain about our new life. Where would I go to school? Would we have a pool at our new home? Would I get to see my dad again? Would I get to see my mom?

The next day at the parade, we snaked our way through the crowd. Vi boosted me onto a mailbox. The noise made my head hurt. Floats cruised, Shriners on tiny bikes, brass bands with bass drums that shook me with each thump. On television, the parade had seemed so happy and benign. In person, however, it was a Technicolor mess.

Vi stood behind me. Occasionally, I'd look back to find her adjusting her scarf or smoking, her jaw clenched in an expression of defense and...anger?

A man behind her with his son perched atop his shoulders knelt to pick up a pennant he'd dropped, rubbing the front of his pants up against Vi's ass as he rose to stand again. He repeated this three times that I saw. Finally, Vi reached back and grabbed him by the crotch.

"Do it again, Mac, and I'll pull it right off," she said. The man backed away. I felt better, safer, after that, and actually enjoyed watching Bullwinkle and company drift above us down Broadway.

Vi and I returned to Piqua the next day, but it changed us. We were even closer than before. She'd shown me bigger worlds. I'd shown her that I felt secure and proud in being her little girl, wherever we were.

Chapter 36

"Macy?" A blur became a blonde.

This wasn't just any blonde. This was...Olide.

Lying in my bed at Chez Schizo, I was pleasantly surprised. Who knew such beauty would reach me beyond
the steel-meshed window glass of the nut house?

I'd met Olide (pronounced Oh-leed, as in, "Oh, lead
me astray") after having a near death experience at an
"asthma spa" attended, you guessed it, at the behest of
my lovely wife.

The first tip that this asthma treatment wouldn't in-
clude a French manicure was its location: the fourth
floor of a four-floor walk-up. Another clue was the live
chicken and subsequent piles of chicken shit that I had
to navigate in the lobby. Once inside this gulag, I was
whisked down a dark corridor, a metal door slammed,
and I was ordered gruffly to strip and sit on benches
cluttered with other wheezers like myself. Only a soli-
tary flickering lightbulb hung from the ceiling and kept
us all from shrieking. This "asthma spa" turned out to
be a makeshift Russian benya, a holy trinity of horrors
that included the inhalation of boiling aromatic steam,
"percussion" (being beaten) with tree branches and then

a hasty release into the snow, or in this case, a tiled room where a "nurse" hosed you with icy water.

Seeing Olide at the funny house brought all of this back.

Olide, sweet Olide, she'd looked so much like Marcia Brady with that hose in her hand that day. Naked and freshly beaten with birch, I pleaded for mercy. She'd held my hand and led me from the fog. I'd thanked her with a business card and a kiss. A deep kiss. A soul kiss. A long kiss. We'd lunched later that week. Nothing more, but...

"Olide." I waved.

She took tiny steps in her little high-heeled shoes. Painful shoes, yes, but there wasn't one practical, orthopedic bone in Olide's body. Young blondes are not built for comfort, but for speed.

"Macy." She gave me that surrendering smile.

I patted the bed beside me. "Come on over, honey."

And so it went, my capitulation to the "Madonna/whore" complex, Faith being the holy mother, and Olide being the...

"Macy." She slid her hand up my thigh and under my gown, reaching out with the other to pull the curtain closed.

With the aid of Olide, I gave the nut house the slip. Robbed of my street clothes by an earlier, surlier staff, Olide raided the hospital lost and found, bringing me a velour jacket the color of piss that read "Dis My Crib" across the front. Still, this left me with my ass hanging out of my gown as I skidded down the hall and into the ambulance bay.

I whipped my head around. No taxis, no nothing. Only an idling ambulance.

Fuck.

Let me stress that I hadn't much of a choice. Not really, anyway. It was a desperate situation, and sometimes, as everyone knows, a situation of such a desperate and complex nature demands extreme action.

Like stealing an ambulance to kidnap your son.

I didn't abuse my power. I didn't turn on the lights or sirens, mostly because I hadn't a clue how to operate them. I did, however, get the hang of the loud speaker.

"I'm not joyriding here, people. And I'm not a crackhead." I spoke into the CB-like microphone. "I'm going to take this thing and park it and leave 100 dollars on the driver's seat for gas and your inconvenience. I just didn't have time to wait around for a taxi. I'm sorry."

And I was, really. Nobody but a total sicko would want to steal an ambulance. Not as if you could jack it up and pimp it out. An ambulance is an ambulance... nothing hip about it. P. Diddy wouldn't be caught dead in an ambulance.

I ditched the ride a mere two blocks down and walked quite leisurely to a park, arriving with no shoes, no pants, but, thankfully, my clutch purse (the one thing that Olide had managed to rescue).

"Fifty dollars!" I yelled up at a trucker who'd parked his rig and was eating his lunch.

"Sorry, lady. Not interested." He continued eating a sloppy sandwich, wiping mayo off his scruffy chin with a dirty-fingernailed forefinger. "I'm married, and besides…" He looked me up and down. "Uh…no thanks."

"For your clothes!" I shouted up at him. "I'll give you fifty dollars and you can keep your underwear!"

He shook his head, but I still had his interest.

"A hundred!"

A pause. A head shake.

"Two!" I waved the cash up at him. "I'll give you two hundred dollars for your clothes!"

As children, in a rare moment of play, my brother, Elliott, had taped teddy-bear hair to my upper lip, dressed me in an army surplus gun belt and sombrero, and taken me trick-or-treating. Instant bandito. It had been the best costume I'd ever donned.

Until now.

I cinched the waist of the jeans, tucked the shirt in behind the "Mustache Rides: five cents" belt buckle, and pulled down the brim of a Miller Beer cap as I called for a cab.

I may look like a Wuornos, but I am a Delong-champ, dammit.

And so is my son.

Chapter 37

Back at the not-so-old homestead, climbing up to peer into a side window, my footing, and my mood, was hardly stable.

"Shit!" A paint can slid out from under my feet. I landed on a wheelbarrow's edge.

"Fuck!" I clutched my side, my cigarette dropping to the brick patio outside our bathroom window.

Immediately, I was pissed. Here I was, lurking outside my own house to steal my own kid. And now, this shit happens.

"Oh, Christ!" I tried to keep it down, gritting my teeth, telling myself to butch up and deal with it. But it hurt. It hurt like a bitch. And I'd frenched enough CPR dummies in first-aid classes to know that ribs are very vulnerable. I was sure I'd cracked one. Maybe two.

"Oh...God." The pain kept thumping away and I started to shake. Shock? Nerves? It didn't matter. This pain wasn't letting up. This pain was going to last for a good long while. It had pitched a fucking tent and built a campfire.

I twisted and groaned.

Fuuuuuuuck.

Neighbors. We had neighbors. Despite the dense thatch of jungle separating us, our neighbors were actually quite close.

Neighbors might have codeine. A neighbor might even be a doctor.

Having ruined our courtship with the lesbian germophobes to our left, I proceeded down a short garden path and knocked on a heavy wooden door.

"Codeine...Vicodin...Morphine...Ecstasy...*anything.*" I moaned a plea, not bothering to look up, initially, to find that...

"Michael?"

...the neighbor was Michael Marks, ex-husband to the late Catherine Marks, former coke buddy and part-time dyke.

He seemed amused, and a little alarmed, to find me playing the poor match girl on his doorstep.

"Macy?" I could tell he was ready to peel off a quip had I not been bent over, clutching my side. He held back, thankfully. "Um...come in."

A former actor in a cheap cologne advertising campaign, Michael had entered the motion-picture industry at the behest of the late Cath. They'd gotten their moment in the sun with a couple of under budget blockbusters, even winning an Oscar for production, but while Cath had blown her dough one little white line at a time, Michael had invested, and from the looks of things, quite wisely. He was still unbelievably handsome in that tan, California way. Since their split, I'd heard he'd dated Cher, in her prime, among others. While with Cath, he'd flirted with me shamelessly. On more than one occasion, I barely resisted his advances.

Then again, during those, the salad days, the Joan Baez ballad days, I'd been perpetually stoned.

So now I sat, or rather curled myself, onto a sofa, easing myself onto the cushions, in too much agony to be embarrassed by the whole scene.

"I'm sorry to present myself like this, Michael," I managed to squeak out. "I believe I've broken a rib."

"Oh...my God...I..." He turned one way, then another. Panicked or...embarrassed? "Let me call for an ambulance."

"No!" The exhalation gave me pain that sent black spots before my eyes. "They may be looking for me, Michael. I kind of...well, I stole an ambulance." He looked justifiably alarmed. "I parked it. I only borrowed it. I mean, so I could get these clothes."

He blinked. "I don't understand."

"Please, Michael," I implored him, feeling queasy and not above utterly begging him. "Please. Please help me."

Per our past, he poured me a bourbon on the rocks to wash down two Flexeril. I thanked him but swallowed them dry. Within minutes I was adrift on his sofa, still hurting, but not enough to keep me from giggling in fascination at how large men's steel-toed work boots made my already big feet appear. My legs stretched out before me, I felt gangly by funhouse proportions.

I am Ichabod Crane with a broken rib, in my neighbor's house, whose late wife I have fucked.

I drowsed for most of an hour, slowly becoming aware of the sweaty stench in my clothes that was not my own. Perhaps I should have chosen something more durable to drape myself in for this adventure: a loin cloth, perhaps, to get me in touch with my more primal side, the Angelina Jolie within.

I sat up to find Michael in mid-sentence.

"...and I never understood why she didn't just bring you home. You know, to be with us both."

Oh, Christ. Leave it to a man to whine about the threesome that got away.

I practiced my routine on the steps leading up to the house. A typical afternoon in California, the sun tickled the tops of the trees. I took a breath of ocean air and readied myself, tits slung low without a bra in my pearl-button Sears Roebuck shirt.

"Ahem..." I made my way, scuffing my boots into the living area. Banky and Delaina sat playing with card-board bricks in front of the fireplace. "I see you two are getting along famously."

And they were. I felt jealousy prick at my spine. She was gorgeous and young, this Delaina, deep tan with blue eyes and a sideways smile. A post-Midwestern transfer surfer. I wondered, studying her, then, if Faith would follow the suit of many a wealthy wench and bed the au pair when the jury was still out on her and me.

"You must be Macy." The model/nanny spoke. I fought a smile, but couldn't help but return hers. "I'm Delaina."

"At last we meet." The chicken hawk in me began to drool. I shook her hand. "I understand our boy has quite a crush."

She blushed. I winked automatically in response.

Me, ever dashing in my saggy-crotched jeans. "Faith forget about his dental appointment?" I asked, moving about the room as if it were mine, not only by deed. "Or did she say she'd make it back by three?"

Delaina's brow wrinkled. "She didn't mention it."

"Ah, no bother. I can take him. Not a problem." Banky had already attached himself to my leg, giggling. "We'll be back in a couple of hours. You can stick around if you like." *That's right. Be cordial, be sweet, be benign.* "Make yourself at home." I chuckled. "Though I haven't had the chance to use them myself, I understand there are tennis courts and a pool around back. Invite a friend over if you like. And" I winked, again, flicking the air whimsically, perverted old fairy that I was. "...you needn't worry about running home for your suit. To swim, that is. We're rather informal here."

She looked at me, lip slightly wrinkled in not-so-slight disgust. Nope, this was a straight one. My veiled kindness had creeped her out, which was, sadly, part of the plan.

And just like that, Banky and I were in the cab and on our way.

I asked the driver to take us to a rental agency...any car rental agency...and then changed my mind. This would only leave an easy trail for the missus to follow, if she chose to. Faith was no idiot. She'd check the airports, the rental agencies, the bars.

So it was out of necessity, really, when I summoned our driver's attention to pull over at a fresh-vegetable stand near the pier. What caught my attention wasn't the melons, for once, but a sagging eggplant-colored pickup

149

truck with the words "The Sheryl Crow" hand painted on the driver's side door.

Cukes, cabbage, and beans, all cluttered the box. A baby-faced forty-something man in a faded Hole concert tee graced the tail. His hat read "Ric," perhaps a misspelling, perhaps an acronym for "running in circles." He bobbed his head hello and spit on the ground.

I cupped my side, hip cocked jauntily. "How much?"

Banky began petting the man's waggy pit bull. I thrust my palm into the pocket of my jeans, fingering my money.

"Two bucks a head. Beans depend on…"

"I mean the truck." I lit a cigarette, furiously flicking my Bic in the breeze. "How much for the truck?"

I was hoping this wasn't one of those "it's a collector's item" assholes, a backyard Donald Trump. I was pleased when he smiled and had an intelligent face behind his beard. "The truck?"

"The truck." *The truck, yes, in all its rusted glory.* "It runs, no?"

He laughed. "Yeah, sure, it runs. It runs pretty good."

Despite being a few years my junior, he looked me up and down.

He's attracted to me. I look like a roadie for Willie Nelson in this getup, and he's attracted me to me still.

I love him for this.

"I didn't really plan on having it up for sale, but…"

"But you will if the price is right, right?" I flashed him a city girl smile and pulled out my wad, counting hundreds until I got to $1,500. "Close?"

"Well, I just bought two new tires."

I start flipping again, this time ending at $2,000. "Closer?"

"Almost."

"Christ on a crutch, guy!" I was pissed, but desperate, counting out another $500. "This is it." I offered a fan of cash. "This and a ride home in the cab for you, the cabbage, and your little black dog."

Come on, motherfucker. Just give me the keys.

"Buster."

"Pleased to meet you, Buster." I kept smiling.

"That's my dog's name." He gave me a funny look. Sensitive. Hurt, even. "Don't you want to know about the name?"

"The name?" I blinked.

"I mean the truck." This was clearly no regular flea market Okie. It seems I'd stumbled upon Mr. Sensitive in a trucker hat. "We named her. Like a boat."

"The Sheryl Crow." I placed the cash in his hand. "Good-looking gal with a lot of miles on her, huh?"

He seemed pleased.

Chapter 38

Rust sifted down from behind the windshield with each bump, the accompaniment to each of my many grunts of pain. Due to boredom or an unseen exhaust leak, Banky had curled up to sleep on the big bench seat beside me, a loose, pre-safety-age buckle belting him into place.

Marcella Antoinette...what the hell are you doing?

I bought a map, Chiclets, cheap sunglasses and Coke at a gas station, pausing briefly in the restroom to use a towel and my buttery new belt to splint my ribs.

Where are we?

I looked at my new, hard-assed image in the driver's side mirror of "The Sheryl Crow."

WHO are we?

"I believe we are the *Dukes of Hazzard*," I said, tweaking my mirrored aviator shades at the temples.

Two hours into our trip and my mobile rang.

Faith.

"Macy, where are you?" From the flat sound of her voice, I could tell she was scared shitless.

GOOD.

"I'm fine, Faith. Banky's fine, too. We just decided to

take a little trip together." I held the phone in his direction. Banky yelled "HI!" and laughed.

"For God's sake, come home."

"See, that's the problem here, kiddo." I cranked the window shut. "I don't have a home. Not yet. But currently we're considering a villa in...South America, maybe?"

"Macy..."

"Perhaps Finland..."

"MACY!"

"Then again, one can't be certain that boy and I won't be seized with this urge for goin' for a long, long time." I cleared my throat, lowering my voice. "Who knows WHEN we'll settle down?"

"Macy, please." She sounded together. A plus. "Please come home. I..."

"I don't have a home..."

Click. End of conversation. Buh-bye.

"What say we find us some grub, boy?" I tousled his hair.

A few hours on the road and suddenly I'm eastbound and dowwwwwn...loaded up and truckin'...

Never much into convenience store sandwiches... you know, the ones one aisle over from the motor oil...I found them to be amazingly palatable. Banky, on the other hand, grumped until I caved in for some chicken lumps from the golden arches. Evening found us both belching and wrung out. I got us a room at a crummy little four star spot in Arizona. The boy snored softly, like his mother, and I sat up most of the night, unable to find a comfortable position or a watchable program on cable.

•

"Mom?" Banky put down his action figures for a moment of seriousness. "When are we going home?"

The kid was getting wise. Our third day on the road and he was questioning the agenda.

"Well, we're going to see your grandma, first," I said, which was news to me.

"Will Faith be there?"

I turned and smiled at him, hands gripping the wheel. "You bet."

For the first time on our adventure, I had a real plan. Make it to Piqua, Ohio, city of my birth, where maybe I could eat, rest, and see a goddamned doctor for my rib. Call Faith. And be headed to New York by the time she flew out to pick up Banky.

Zero confrontation. Perfect.

It wasn't a bad plan. Judging from my lack of codeine, it seemed to be the best plan, for both me and the boy.

Somewhere in Indiana, I spied button-flies of appropriate size, a work shirt, and a denim jacket on a clothes line. I quietly made my purchase, pinning a fifty to the nylon rope, changing out of my sink-washed grubbies in a gas station bathroom.

Banky and I reached Piqua city limits by nightfall. I pulled off to the side of the road and smoked a cigarette as my boy napped in the front seat of the truck.

I don't recall driving to my father's house, or to Lorraine's. Like a blackout without the booze, I'd just appeared in an armchair, still foggy/headachy from a nap and enjoying the warmth from the fireplace as it soaked through my clothes. Ah, my childhood home. I could smell something cooking.

A green log snapped and startled me. I sprang to my feet.

"Shit!" I looked at my wristwatch. Dead. A fucking Cartier and it was dead.

"Macy?" A woman's voice. Was it Lorraine? Was it Vi? Had I officially lost my mind? Again?

I was searching the foyer closet for my coat, the magical Levi's jacket that held my cigs, when my father's third wife, now widow, caught me by the arm.

"Are you all right?"

"Lorraine!" I jumped. "Yes! I am!" Then, more calmly…"I'm fine." I continued my search. "So…how are you?"

She looked good, Lorraine, much better than she had at Dad's funeral. Still in shape, still blonde still young. From a look around, Wild Bill had left her with enough to live comfortably, if not extravagantly. Her surroundings, like herself, were lovely, sensible, and definitely the best available within reason.

"I'm well. Um…" She patted my arm and spoke slowly, soothingly, the way you'd speak to a cornered animal before slamming a net over its head. Appropriately. "Come sit and have something to eat, okay? Come on…"

"How long did I sleep?"

"You were here when I got here. I'm not sure." She smiled, coaxing me, but careful not to touch. "Come on. Let's eat."

It was beginning to come back. Everyone in Ohio leaves their doors open. I think it's on the state flag, a crude rendering of a front door flung open to the world. In my dry drunken state, I'd simply slipped in and crashed on the first soft furniture I could find.

"Where's Banky?"

"Oh, your Mom came by with Elliott. I had to run out for a few and she volunteered to watch him." She smiled sheepishly. "Sorry, I thought she'd just stay here with him, but…"

"YOU LET MY MOTHER AND MY FUCKING DRUG FIEND OF A BROTHER TAKE MY LITTLE BOY???"

And just then, just like in the movies, my mobile phone rang.

Unknown caller.

"Miz Deelawnshamp?"

It was a man. A man with a bad fake southern accent.

Adam Sandler?

"Yes?"

"We have yer sun. We'll need a million dollars in cash to give him back safe and sound." He cleared his throat the way only a true redneck could do, a big, phlegm-sucking noise. The hillbilly accent might be fake, but the rest was pure…

"Elliott?"

"Uh…" A pause, a sound of muffled talk. "Call you right back."

"Well, that's just great." I shook my head, still holding the phone open and in hand. "Elliott's kidnapped Banky."

And so it was.

I let myself fall back into a chair and told Lorraine my tale of woe.

"Let me get this straight." She frowned, genuinely

confounded. "You kidnapped your son. Then Elliott kidnapped him from you after you."

"Yes."

"He's your son, but you're not his mother. He was taken by your brother."

"I'm supposed to be becoming his mother, legally. Elliott's my biological brother."

Such a simple situation, so hard to explain to Lorraine.

"But his mother isn't his mother? And your brother is his uncle?"

Who's on first?

"His mother is his birth mother. I'm his..."

"Other mother!" She smiled. "Got it!"

"Right."

"And now you've split up?" She reached across the table and touched my hand. "Oh, honey, I'm so sorry. But you can't just go around kidnapping a baby..."

"I know." I hung my head. "But the thought of only seeing him every other weekend...I couldn't stand it."

"Shouldn't you contact the police about Elliott?"

"Absolutely not." I folded my arms. "I can't take any risks with this. I'll give him his money. I just want Banky back."

Lorraine raised an eyebrow. "Banky?"

"We named him William Behnke Delongchamp, after both of our fathers." I conjured an image of Banky in my mind and, for a moment, couldn't see the details of his face. This quick, and I was forgetting?

"Your father would have been so happy."

Especially if he knew that one of his seed had filtered down into my wifey.

Chapter 39

"So you're in a fix, are you?" My mother raised one eyebrow, a physical ability we seemed to share. "I should have known this wasn't just a visit to see your old mother. You never have given half a shit about me. I know that."

"Mom…" My voice cracked. I cleared my throat. "Where is he? Where's Elliott?"

"Why?" Ever the mother hen, I saw the look of automatic defense snap into place on her face like always when it came to her baby boy.

"Because I have a good idea that Elliott…" *Whoa. Be careful, here.* "…that Elliott may be able to help me find out who took my son."

"You know, he doesn't even talk to those people, anymore. The ones from the prison. He told me he went in to get a can of Skoal at the gas station and when he came out…poof…your little boy was gone." She frowned. "I'm sure he didn't have a thing to do with it, Marcella."

"I know. I'm sure he doesn't." *Jesus Christ.* "But I think…I might need his help."

"Never fails." She shook her head, smirking. "Like that doctor says on the TV, family can't be replaced. They're the ones you always turn to in a bind."

"I guess so." I sat in a kitchen chair, my legs rubbery. I was too tired to be angry with her usual bull.

"Old Violet Rogers can't help you this time, can she?" she said, opening a cupboard door. "Coffee?"

"Sure." Vi. I shut my eyes hard. Vi, my illustrious step-mother. Vi would have known what to do, would have held me, would have helped me hunt down my fucking bastard of a brother. But Vi was gone, and I remembered walking on the beach with my boy, the question first coming to me then: Would I be strong enough for Banky, as Vi had been for me?

The question came to me now, and made me set my feet flat against the linoleum floor. Yes. Yes, I would be. I had to be.

"I never could understand how your father got past that scar." Mom sat a thick coffee cup before me. I took it and nodded politely in thanks. "I'll admit she was a good-looking woman, but Violet Rogers was nothing but an old, worn out whore." Enter my mother, the fixator. She ran her hand from the front of her left ribs to the back. "She had a great big scar that ran from here to here. And your father was funny about those things."

The scar. I'd seen it when Vi and I had changed together to go swimming on numerous occasions. It ran like a crooked railroad track from underneath her left breast around to nearly reach her spine. The scar, a relic from the 1950s mandatory pneumonectomy following her second bout with tuberculosis. Vi, the Texas one-lunger.

"Mother..."

"He got bored with her, I know that," she snorted. "I went over there the last year she was alive, I remember, to leave some socks I'd mended for your father, and she was right there on the floor. The great Violet Rogers, and she couldn't carry herself to the bathroom."

Suddenly, my mother's tone changed. She dropped her shoulders. She softened. "She was just a little thing, weak as a kitten. What could I do?" Her eyes became shiny and distant. "You were in school. God only knows where he was off to. She had nobody else."

Vi's last year with us had been a hard one. She'd spent most of the winter in bed, sick with fevers and fighting any flu that floated into town. I hadn't wanted to remember her this way, but here it was. Obviously, my mother had been witness to more than I'd thought. And obviously, somehow, she cared.

"I said to him, 'Bill, that woman needs to be in a hospital.' He said she was too stubborn to go." My mother dabbed at her eyes with a dish towel, still avoiding my gaze. "If she hadn't been sleeping with Dr. Greenbaum on the side, he would have never made house calls and she wouldn't have lasted as long as she did. Your father didn't give a damn if she lived or died." She said it angrily, sympathetically, thoroughly disgusted. Mom may have hated Vi, but she hated Dad more for turning his back on her. Even my mother had some mother still in her.

"What the hell are you talking about?" I stood, the blood rushing to my face and neck. "He DID care. He loved Vi."

I didn't need this. I didn't need to know this about

Vi, that she'd fucked Dr. Greenbaum, that my mother had been her wet nurse the week before her death.

"Mom…" I began, making an effort to maintain control.

My mother finally looked at me squarely, her hands firmly on her hips. "Your father loved Vi like he loved every other woman…when it was convenient."

Look at me: a chip off the old cock.

"Mom…" I not only felt the blood rush now…I felt it bubble, bubble, toil and trouble.

"God knows I loved him…"

"Mom…" Count down: ten, nine, eight…

"If you only knew the sacrifices I made…"

That's it.

"AAAAAAAAGHHHHHH!" I yanked at my hair and stamped my feet, at last standing somewhat bow-legged and ready for battle, fists clenched and wild-eyed. "Mother! This is NOT about you! Or Dad! Or anyone else! This is about my child!"

She folded her arms and snickered. "Temper, temper…"

And I rushed in for the kill.

"You listen to me, old woman." It was a voice I didn't know I had in me, a whispering, desperate hiss. I had her by the upper arms now, my face only inches from hers. "You give me Elliott's address, and you give it to me quick, and we will never, ever, have to see each other again. *Capice?*"

Her eyes welled up. Fear? *Good!* "Marcella…"

But I was not Marcella anymore. I was not the kid who watched her moods swing to and fro. I was only Banky's mom. And I was pissed.

"You give it to me, or believe me, I'll tear this house apart until I find it."

And there it was, the shift of power, that great and pitiful moment when you realize that you are bigger and scarier, at last, than the big and scary woman from your childhood.

"H-he doesn't have a phone." Surprise. "He'll be bringing his family to the live nativity here in Piqua tonight."

My mother pulled away from me and I felt guilty for putting my hands on her. For about three seconds.

"Thank you." I felt queasy, clammy. How long had it been since I'd eaten? Slept more than three hours?

"It's Christmas Eve."

"Well…" I sighed, turning on my heel toward the door. "Merry Christmas."

"Merry Christmas, Macy."

Suddenly, I felt disappointed for not carrying a photo of my son.

"He's your grandson, you know." I smiled, stepping toward her for the moment. Mom didn't look up until I said, "His name is Bill."

And she flushed, smiling before she could stop herself.

"Really?" She stepped toward me. "Elliott has two girls, Charlene and Darlene."

Leave it to Elliott to come up with names that only a country-western act could be proud of.

"Well, this one's definitely a boy." I folded my arms to keep from reaching for her, an impulse I was not particularly proud of. "And his name is Bill." So we stood for a moment, enjoying the bridge-building magic that only a kid can bring. I turned to leave.

162

"You have a coat?" She opened a closet door. "Here, go on." She handed me a pink monstrosity. "I know, I know. It's ugly. But it's goose down. It's warm." She nodded, insistent. "Go on. You can't be traipsing around without a coat."

Outside, I felt a twinge in my chest, a skip.

Holy shit. My mother loves me. I grew up to be a big lesbo, I half-threatened her and still, she loves me.

I made it to the driver's door of the truck before I got the spins.

"Fuck." I said it aloud and inside my head. *Fuck.*

I envied, then, the people of the planet who had faith, who believed. The girl at Columbine who had believed in the face of certain death. The passengers holding hands in prayer on the deck of the Titanic. Office workers holding hands as they leapt from the World Trade Center. Brave people. Why didn't I believe like them? Why couldn't I, as the bumper sticker says, just "Let go and let God"?

I closed my eyes and steadied myself. The twinge disappeared.

I looked up. The sky had ceased its spinning.

Please don't let Banky die for my sins. I transmitted to any deity listening. Phyllis Delongchamp still loves me, her black sheep. Miracles can happen. So, please. Please, let me find my baby.

The first thing I did was throw out my cigarettes. The second was to procure a hat and scarf at the local Quickie Mart. If I was to capture Banky, I had to stay healthy and at the top of my game.

Swinging open the door to "The Sheryl Crow," I heard panting.

"Mother of shit!" I jumped back, startled by the land mass with a tongue that had snuck up behind me.

Holy fuck.

This wasn't just a dog. This was a rottweiler, and it looked hungry.

I slammed the truck into reverse and started to flee, but I couldn't. Graying and abused, collar grown into her neck, she looked pitiful. She reminded me of, well, me.

Whatever you do, don't get out of the truck. These are the dogs that kill people for kicks. These dogs are built to maim. You've seen the headlines, dumbass. Run! Speed away before you become Rottkill!

She gave me a crocodile glance: the slow, steady gaze only predators give to prey. Then, just as I was about to back away from my certain peril, she smiled. A real smile. A dog smile. A smile like you see on Iams calendars.

"What do you want?" I sighed. "I don't do dogs, honey. I'm not one of those touchy feely animal types, and as for bestiality, I've read the run-down on it in that fucking Patrick Califia book, and no matter how long your tongue is, it ain't for me. So run along. Go on."

She stayed. And smiled.

I reached over to open the passenger door. No need to whistle. In two limping attempts, she'd pulled herself in, settled into the seat beside me, and ripped a noxious fart.

"Well, that settles it." I undid the collar from around her massive neck. "We're calling you Ripley."

Chapter 40

The Piqua town square sat at the meeting of three churches: Lutheran, Methodist, and Catholic, not necessarily in that order. Growing up, we'd been heathens, lost souls, a.k.a. non-denominational and just fine that way, thank you. God only knew, no pun intended, what faith Elliott and his clan had chosen to cling to. Perhaps St. Bubba the Ex-Con had provided them with direction.

I parked behind Shirl's Lunch Hut, chief concession source in the town square. Said parking spot gave me perfect backstage access to the live nativity, kept me privy to the coming and going action of all three churches, and ensured that an ample supply of steamed wienies and stale buns was close by. A vision in salt stains and loose bondo, its bumper littered with Nascar stickers, the truck gave me enough proper Midwestern disguise to avoid any altercations with the local deputy dawg.

Hank Nichol (known to us in high school as "Nichol the Pickle," for his reputably bumpy, baby gherkin of a wang) cruised by and never flinched. I sat waiting for hours, Ripley at my side, starting and running "The

Sheryl Crow" long enough to stay warm and get a fine carbon monoxide headache brewing.

Rip stared dully at the landscape of snow and dirty footsteps, grumbling upon occasion at the stray parishioner stumbling and sliding in their slick-bottomed church shoes. I began counting folks as they headed to church and stopped at 200. A busy day at the pulpit, a real occasion for pinch-hitting pastors. I wondered aloud if this was a new attendance record for Piqua, seeing that so many machine shops and mom and pop businesses had been forced to close. Eyeing my Midwestern countrymen, I conjectured if they'd been given a little something extra to pray for from President Bush this Christmas. Like food on the table.

"I don't give a great big goddamn what the Bradshaws think."

The words were spit out by a short-haired blond cruising along in boot-cut jeans. She marched through the snow with another woman who didn't look at all like her, but they had the same gait. They must have been sisters.

"Now, Edith…"

"If I want to let someone have an early look at the rummage sale, I'll let them know." She huffed. "They don't just show up the day before and expect to get in. I gave that slut daughter of theirs a kitten and she let it get worms. So as far as I'm concerned…"

Her words trailed off as I watched them sidestep all three churches and head up the street. I smiled, slightly awed by a rarity in Ohio: atheist hard-core garage sale enthusiasts.

"I can't do this, Rip." I stared at the white flesh of my hands, bony fingers wrapped tautly around the steering. "I can't. My chest hurts. I'm tired. I'm not fit for this sort of taxing quest."

And then, much like the voice of Cher, it came: "Pussy."

I jerked erect. "What?"

"You heard what I said." Her lips didn't move, but it was coming from that enormous head. It was Rip. The dog. Speaking to me. My God...was I like that Son of Sam murderer, getting advice from a dog?

"I called you a pussy, because that's what you've become. Just another pussy who'll back down at the first sign of..."

"You got that right." This time the voice came from the opposite direction. A familiar voice, slightly muffled. "A first class, grade A pussy with fries on the side, extra mayo."

Yep. Leaning up against the truck, lips pressed to my window glass, was Vi.

"Now a dog AND my dead step-mother are talking to me." I covered my ears. "La! La! La! La..."

"Cut that shit out, will ya?" Rip nudged me with her nose.

I felt my breath quicken. Panic.

"It's...hmmn mrrrr..." Vi knocked on the window, motioning for me to crank it down. I did. "Your inhaler. It's in your coat pocket." She smirked. "Nice coat, by the way. Never would have caught me dead in such a thing."

"Me, either," Rip muttered.

"This is all your fault!" I screamed at Vi, taking a puff. "You're the one who told me to kidnap him."

Rip snorted. "Just like you to blame somebody else…"

"Well, goddammit, you had to do *something*." Vi thumped her fist on the windshield, sending a rain of rust into my lap. "Besides, everything would have been just fine if you hadn't fallen asleep."

"Okay! All right!" I yanked at my hair. "This is just too much!"

"Go ahead. Have a nervous breakdown." Rip scratched at her neck with her hind leg. "That'll help matters."

Three o'clock and I still hadn't seen Elliott. Eager to escape being hounded by a hound as well as by Vi, I came to a decision. I made my way through the double doors of the largest church first. Being Christmas Eve, the joint was packed, and after swinging open the heavy side door of the place, I knew I'd be lucky to find a seat. Growing up, my hometown had always been flush with Catholics.

All you can eat Friday fish fries kept many a mom and pop diner in business, and after assessing the parish, I could see that little had changed. There were the Finches, the Nepolitanos, the Carsons, the Baileys. Growing up as a non-denominational heathen, I hoped that I'd blend in and not be recognized as I made my way into the flock. Being a six foot tall woman in a pink Michelin Man-style coat, buff-shined wing tips, mirrored gas station aviator sunglasses, and a bright orange cap with flaps might make me look like a suspicious retard in New York, but in Ohio it was a familiar costume and I was sure to be embraced as one of their own.

Besides, the whole purpose had been to keep warm and dry and not succumb to my customary susceptibility. I couldn't afford to catch cold and wither. I was on a mission here, and I had to be strong.

I am not returning to that truck without Banky. Fuck no.

As I faced the enormous, tortured Jesus suspended behind the podium, I realized it wasn't Him I had a beef with. It was his Old Man. Hands clasped and head bowed, I sent my silent question to the entity above.

How could you sacrifice your only son?

I raised my head and surveyed the flock surrounding me.

If letting Christ die a horrible death was to save mankind, I don't think it was worth it.

How many of these good people of the church had stolen? Cheated?

Coveted thy neighbor's young wife in the shower through a set of binoculars? And how could it all be erased by a take-a-number confessional? It didn't make any sense to be given carte blanche and still get into heaven if you repented at the last minute. It seemed like a loophole, like some plea bargain attempt by a sleazy soul-saving attorney. I could see the pitchman on a cheap late-night infomercial barking "Sin all you like! Confess once a year! What a value, what a deal!"

1-800-call-Judas.

I scratched my head.

Do these people actually believe this, or do they just WANT to believe?

Perhaps they had it right, but I didn't think so.

Is this really what Christianity is all about? Or is it all just for show, a bad Christmas parade?

I let my eyes drift across the backs of heads. Necks thick like tree trunks. Slim necks with tendons standing out, a dent between them. Delicate question marks of hair at the bases of men's skulls. Shaggy home perms. Collars of polyester coats. The occasional mink making its appearance after a year in storage.

Ugh.

And it was three rows up that I saw the tip of a dragon's tail emerging from a stiff shirt collar.

Elliott!

Instinctively, I shot up out of my seat.

The priest continued his spiel.

"The Lord be with you."

Son of a bitch!

"And also with you," baaed the sheep.

A very conservative-looking older fellow with white hair and a Burberry scarf turned to me.

"Peace be with you," he said, smiling, extending his hand.

I nodded. "And also with you?"

He turned and sat. Obviously, I'd given a fair facsimile of the Catholic secret handshake.

I moved toward the edge of the pew, crushing a few toes as I went and not bothering to apologize. No time for that.

The priest continued: "Lord God almighty, in the unity of the Holy Spirit, all glory and honor are yours..."

Reaching the aisle at last, I felt my knees pop in a semi-arthritic genuflection.

I grunted. "Shit."

A woman toting a cheap handbag shot me a disgusted look.

Fuck off, house frau. This is serious.

And the voices rising around me provided cover, allowing me to travel toward Elliott in stealth: "I confess to almighty God, and to you, my brothers and sisters…"

My pulse pounded in my ears. *Elliot, you bastard, where is my baby?*

"…that I have sinned through my own fault, in my thoughts and in my words, in what I have done, and in what I have failed to do; and I ask blessed Mary, ever virgin, all the angels and saints, and you, my brothers and sisters, to pray for me to the Lord, our God."

By just being here amongst the brethren, do I qualify for moral amnesty?

At last I was directly behind him, leaning close to his left ear, close enough to spit on the dragon's tail. "You tell me where my boy is or so help me God I'll kill you."

"…Amen."

"He's not here," Elliot whispered out of the corner of his mouth. I could see his stained teeth, smell the Budweiser on his breath. "You meet me at the live nativity in an hour, with the money, and you'll get him back. You got the money?"

"Yes," I lied. I didn't have the money. I didn't have anything but a few hundred dollars, a stray rottweiler, and…the gun. Elliott's gun. Lavinia had shipped a great deal of my belongings from New York. Elliott's gun was packed right along with them. I'd grabbed it in desperation when I swiped Banky. It, along with a half-eaten bag of corn chips and assorted maps, was stashed beneath the seat of the truck.

Guns are heavier than you'd think. In the movies, characters tuck them into their waistbands and coat pockets like they're as light as plastic combs, but this is simply not the case. Guns are heavy. They should be. If not, more people would probably be inclined to carry them.

"Marlboro Lights." I slapped a five down on the counter of the Quickie Mart. A smiling little fellow in a clean orange smock gave me my change.

"Is that all I can do for you, Ken?"

"Huh?"

"I see your name there." He pointed. "On your shirt."

"Oh!" I laughed. "Yes." Two days in a dirty work shirt and no makeup and I was passing for a man? Egads. "Nothing else, thanks."

"I'm Fred." He grabbed my hand and shook it vigorously. "Going to be a cold night, eh, Ken?"

"Yup. Sure looks that way." I pulled my hand back and moved for the door. "Well, I should be going."

"Have a good night!" Fred's voice trailed after me.

A crowd had already begun to gather at the manger when Rip and I arrived.

"Well, this is it," I said, heart pounding as I shut off the ignition.

Rip sat in silence, watching the crowd.

I held the pistol in my hand. "I don't even know how to use this."

Rip panted.

"What, no advice?"

Snow crunched beneath my loose work boots as I made my way through the chatting townsfolk. A closer view of the festivities revealed that Elliott was not only meeting me at the live nativity, he *was* the live nativity. My brother stood holding a staff beneath the glow of coffee-can floodlights. His wife, Baby, was draped in a SpongeBob sheet, kneeling in prayer. And my boy lay on a mound of straw, looking confused.

I leaned in close to the donation box. "Psst! Elliott!"

And then I did it. I pulled the gun. A collective gasp came over the crowd as they moved back.

"That man stepped on my feet at church today!" a woman shrieked.

"Don't do it, Ken!" I heard from behind me.

Elliott gawked. "That's my gun!"

"That's my son!" I blurted.

"Mom!" Banky ran and attached himself to my leg. Elliott froze, his hands held high. Deputy Hank Nichol the Pickle arrived post haste. And somewhere in the distance, I could swear the North Star was shining.

Chapter 41

They're right, whoever wrote the song. It's *not* easy being green.

"Ow!" I fussed as Lila Patch, head of the Piqua Pride Christmas float committee, glued plastic rhinestones to my face. Covered head to toe in verdigris makeup and spray-painted tinfoil, I was intended to resemble the Statue of Liberty on Piqua Pride's "Christmas in New York" float. Eyeing my reflection in a hand mirror, I looked more like that genie from *Pee-wee's Playhouse*.

"Mecca lecca hi, mecca hiney ho." I crunched my glittered hair. "Why the hell am I doing this again?"

Lila smiled sweetly. "Because you're a nice person."

I struggled to light a cigarette. "And?"

"And you wrecked the live nativity."

"And?"

"And you don't want to be banished from returning to your home town."

"So that's why I'm in this friggin' pole barn." I nodded, still spying my reflection with one hand. "My God, I'm Kermit the Dyke."

"Mom!"

Banky ran at me from across the barn floor. Seeing me up close, he recoiled and went screaming back to Faith and Lorraine.

"Banky! It's me!" I stood, cig dangling from my lips, huffing to anyone within earshot. "Can somebody please give me a fucking light?"

The boy ceased his crying. He turned. "Mom?"

Scooping him into my arms, I twirled and laughed.

"See, I told you." Lorraine elbowed Faith. "Can you believe this?"

Pausing to take in the train wreck that was me for a moment, they burst out laughing for a solid three minutes.

"Holy shit, Macy, I've never seen you look so…" Faith pointed, doubled over. "Deciduous."

"Great. Thanks." I ruffled the boy's hair and plunked him on the floor. "I'm glad that someone finds this outfit entertaining."

Lorraine snickered. "So, where's your torch?"

Said torch, a swath of flame-retardant white fabric that resisted all efforts at paint, lay like a gigantic joint against my chair. I lifted it and smiled.

Faith and I locked eyes. Silence.

"I think we'll go get an elephant ear." Lorraine took Banky by the hand. "Why don't you two talk? We'll meet up with you outside."

Alone with her, I felt naked. What could I say?

"Faith, I'm sorry." I bowed my head. "I truly…"

"Just…stop." She shook her head, struggling for words, herself. "If I'd known…"

"It's just that I couldn't bear with not seeing him…"

"Macy, I…I just…" Her voice began to waver. "I

don't know what I'm supposed to do here. I mean, the best thing would probably be..."

"Faith, please..."

"Look." She closed her eyes, steeling herself. "What you did was stupid, it was dangerous, it..."

"Faith..."

"Just...just shut up for a minute, will you?" She clenched her fists, took a breath, then relaxed. "Look, I know it was wrong to take Banky away from you like that. I know it was. But, my God, Macy, you scared me to death! How could you do something so stupid? So reckless?"

"I...I wasn't thinking." Which was true. "I couldn't lose him, you know? I mean, it was bad enough, having to face the prospect of losing you, but both you AND Banky? I couldn't..." I held back my tears. "I'm sorry, Faith. I know it was a mistake. I know that I'm incredibly lucky that this whole situation didn't end in some horrific manner. Hell, I'm lucky you'll still speak to me after what I've done..."

"Macy..."

"I've failed you as a spouse. I've failed Banky. I've failed myself." I sank to my knees. "But please. I did keep one major promise to you. I haven't drank. I haven't drank at all, and believe me, I've wanted to..."

"Macy..."

"I love you. And if you still love me." Tears cut through the makeup on my cheeks. "If you still love me, you'll take your time, but you'll think about us. About me and you. About our family."

Disgusted by my own drama, I sighed. "God, look at me. Just look at me, for crying out loud." I shook my head. "I'm begging you. On my knees. I have no pride, Faith. I'll go to counseling. I'll go on the nicotine patch. I'll go to an AA meeting every fucking day if you like. On my life, I swear, I'll never hurt you this way again."

Faith stepped toward me, then looked away. "I love you, Macy. I can't help that. I can't." She sniffled. "But I don't know if we can work this out."

I swallowed hard. "I'll understand if you can't forgive me, but..." I stood. "Please think about it. Give it some time. Six months, a year...whatever. But please think it over."

"I will." She nodded. "Our flight leaves this afternoon, so..."

"So I'll be seeing you, I guess." I smiled.

"I'll call you when we land." She smiled back. "We'll talk about how we can work things out for you to see Banky."

Faith turned to leave and I whistled. "Hey."

She spun around. "Yeah?"

"Merry Christmas, Faith."

She smiled. "Merry Christmas."

And I watched her walk away, disappearing out into the frozen afternoon.

"So here's a picture of me and Joe at Buffalo Wild Wings."

Lorraine sat at the foot of the bed. Her nurse friend, Shane, an impeccably dressed brunette, stood beside her, holding a photo. "This is just before he whipped his dick out."

"No, he didn't!" Lorraine gasped.

"Oh, yes, yes, he did." Shane tossed her hair and smiled. "Just the kind of guy he is. He pulls his dick out in bars and wears knickers when he golfs. And this is my future husband." She eyed the photo again and frowned. "My face is so big. In every picture I take, I look like some big-faced puppet or something."

"Oh, you do not. You look lovely."

And she did. I moaned in approval, a thermometer still under my tongue.

"One hundred and one," Shane tsked. "Looks like you're not going anywhere today, missy."

I rolled my eyes. "Oh, please. I'm fine. It's a head cold, sugar." I sat up. "I have a thousand things to get in order, so…"

"Not so fast." Lorraine pushed me back. "It's going to take at least a day or two before your things are back in New York. Faith's sending some of your clothes out FedEx, but still…" She patted my hand firmly.

"No jet-setting for you just yet."

A phone rang in the hall. Lorraine fetched it and returned. "It's for you."

"Faith?"

She shook her head. "Trish."

TRISH?

I cleared my throat. "Hello?"

"I'm sorry."

"Huh?"

"I said I'm sorry." She huffed, a tad annoyed at having to repeat herself. "I'm sorry I blamed you for Kate's…gayness, or whatever. I thought I'd get that out of the way."

I was stunned. "Okay, then."

"And if you don't want to talk with me, I understand, but after I opened an e-mail from my mother this morning to find you riding a float in the Piqua Christmas parade, well..." She laughed. "I couldn't resist calling."

I sighed. "Not one of my finer moments."

"Why were you holding a giant joint?"

"That was supposed to be my torch. Obviously, there were a great deal of budget constraints." I swung my feet over the edge of the bed. "Then again, this town could use a couple of deep tokes, so I guess it was appropriate."

"Still Piqua, huh?"

I smiled. "Still Piqua."

A pause.

"Mace?"

"Yeah, hon?"

"I really am sorry." Her voice softened. "I acted like an asshole."

"Yes, you did," I said, still happy at hearing from her, but still hurt.

"So, um...may I ask..." She snickered. "Why were you the fucking Statue of Liberty in the Piqua Christmas parade?"

I sighed. "I was the fucking Statue of Liberty because, well..." I found my handbag on the bedside table and searched for a smoke. "I sort of ruined the live nativity."

"Oh, this has got to be good." She was settling in. "Please elaborate."

I lit my cig and took a drag. "I kidnapped Banky."

"What?!"

"And then Elliott kidnapped him from me." I took another sharp inhalation and wheezed, feeling the catch in my ribcage. "It's rather complicated, but let's just say that I held Elliott at gunpoint." I paused. "He was Joseph."

"I see."

"And then Lila Patch, who turned out to be a huge bull dyke..."

"Surprise."

"...asked me to be on the pride float." I smirked. "Piqua has a fucking gay pride float. Can you believe it?"

"Stranger yet, you were their beloved representative, wrapped in plastic."

"Aluminum foil." I said. "Get it right."

"So now you've got another cold."

"Precisely." I huffed. "And a broken rib. And probably pinkeye from communing with these townsfolk."

"What's with the rib?"

"I wiped out trying to look in a window. Lorraine's drugged me up to ease things a bit, but that's about all one can do for a broken rib."

"You're lucky you didn't break a hip, old girl."

"Fuck you."

We laughed together.

"Our neighbor, you know, the hermit? The one I told you about?"

"Umm, hmm."

"She fell in the shower and broke her neck. And DIED."

"Jesus!"

"I know!" Trish clanged a pot, obviously multi-tasking while she talked with me. "Nobody saw her for a couple of days. When they found her...yeesh." She clanged another pot or plate. "Not pretty."

"That's going to be me, soon enough."

"Dead?"

"Alone." I stubbed out my cig in a rather delicate-looking dish where Lorraine had parked my spare change. "Faith and I are in a period of re-evaluation."

"She dumped you."

"Pretty much, yeah."

"I'm sorry." She sounded genuinely so. "I take it this is related to the kidnapping."

"We split in California and she wasn't going to let me see Banky." I sneezed. "I flipped."

"Gesundheit," she continued. "And Elliott took him."

"Yep. Demanded money. The whole deal." I reached for my cigarettes. "Amazingly, Banky's fine. And Faith's fine."

"And you're not."

"No." I started to cry. "I'm not fine at all."

"Macy..."

"I've lost my wife and baby, I'm sick, and I don't think I'll ever get this glitter out of my hair!"

"Baby, it's okay," she soothed. "Everything will work out."

"And what if it doesn't?" I sniffled. "What if I never see either of them ever again? My life is over! It's over!"

"It's not, honey. It's not," Trish lied. "Why don't you stay with us when you come back to New York? You don't have to stay in that lonely apartment."

"What, so I don't die and go undiscovered for a week?"

A pause.

"Yeah, well, it would be kind of difficult to air out the place."

I stopped crying. I laughed.

"How's Kate?"

"Well, she dropped that Jackie Krepps." Trish didn't sound that relieved at saying this. "But…"

"But what?"

"She's joined this church," she said with disgust. "They've promised to…ahem…'turn her straight.'"

I waited, wondering if I really should say it, then…

"It won't work."

Trish paused, then answered. "I know."

"So…"

"So." She clapped her hands. "How's the drinking coming along?"

"It isn't." I smiled. "I'm not. I mean, I haven't."

She was impressed. "Really?"

"Really."

"You've been through all this and haven't had a drink?"

"Not one drop." I was a little impressed, myself.

"W-wow," Trish stuttered in shock. "Congratulations, Mace. I'm proud of you. I really am."

I coughed and thumped my chest. "Thanks." I coughed again.

"Fuck, this rib is killing me! God knows how many valium she's slipped me, and it still hurts like a bitch."

"You're smoking again, huh?"

I lowered my voice, ashamed. "Yeah."

"Pretty obvious. You've got that whole Suzanne Pleshette thing going on."

I giggled. "And that's a bad thing?"

"Not if you're Suzanne Pleshette. Why don't you get Germaine to give you some of those patches when you come back? Hal has a few patients who've tried them. A few have had success."

"I'll consider it. Anything's better than the gum. Yech!"

"I guess the patches give you weird dreams, though."

"I dreamed last night that Kenny Rogers was in my stomach," I said. "Can't get much weirder than that."

Trish laughed. "Uh...no. I guess not. Um...Mace?"

"Yeah?"

"I love you."

"I know." I smiled. "I love you, too."

"Come home," she said. "I worry about you, you know?"

"I know."

"I miss you." Great. Now she was crying. "I'm sorry for how I treated you."

"Yeah, well, you were just worried about your little girl, and I am the ambassador to Queerland."

She laughed. "Just come home, okay?"

"Okay." I laughed, tossing my cigarettes back into my bag. "Okay."

Chapter 42

New York may be the city that never sleeps, but upon my return, it seemed more the city that never sleeps...with me. Somehow, the sober, family-friendly new Macy had unwittingly been drenched in pussy repellent. I tried the bars, but somehow the clientele at Pete's and its ilk didn't seem as savory without beer goggles. I tried cyberfucking, but I found myself unable to type with one hand. I tried bookstores, but those cruising the women's section seemed more familiar with activism and less familiar with personal grooming than I was.

In one last valiant effort to get back on the whore and shrug off my baggage, I signed up for an online dating service. Date one was RUBBERGIRL69, a "horny film student seeking an older sugar mama."

Perfect. She showed up in camouflage parachute pants and a new "retro" Debbie Harry t-shirt. Her hair was blue, and she had a number of visible piercings.

Figuring I had a clue when it came to current culture and that I fit the bill of what she'd advertised for, I shook off my initial repulsion and gave it a go.

"What's your favorite flavor of Jolly Rancher?" she asked.

Quite an icebreaker.

"Green apple, I suppose," I played along. I mean, it's not like Faith had been a Rhoads scholar.

"I like to hide them in my pussy," she chirped.

"Lovely." I smiled, opening a menu. "Shall we order?"

An hour later and she was puking in the parking lot of the restaurant. And not just puking. RUBBERGIRL69 managed to ralph up two bottles of very, very good merlot when obviously I could have gotten away with Riunite.

Date two was hardly an improvement.

"I can see, in your eyes, you've been through so much pain," said Thea, a thirty-two-year-old belly dancer and mystic. In her ad, she'd listed herself as a "stable professional."

"The path to enlightenment is before you." She lifted her arms, knocking over a carafe of ice water and pissing off our waiter. "Open up your heart to me, Macy, and I'll show you the way."

I stood, exasperated.

"The only 'way' I need to be shown is the way out of here." I slipped our server a tip and followed his pointing finger toward the exit.

So upon failing after three strikes, I gave up.

"Look at you!" Trish huffed alongside me, raising the incline on her treadmill. "Twenty full minutes and you're not requiring defibrillation! Go you!"

"Go me. Yeah, well, I've nothing better to do." I kept on at my healthy clip. "Besides, I've gotta keep up with a five-year-old now. Can't have the little shit leaving me in the dust at Toys 'R' Us."

"How very domestic of you," she giggled. "So what's new on the girl front?"

"Girl? What's a girl?" I huffed. "It's been so long since I've seen a pussy, I'd probably throw rocks at it if I did."

Trish laughed. "You mean the great Stud Delongchamp is retiring her assless chaps?"

"Fags wear assless chaps, not dykes," I corrected. "And I...uh...I'm not really interested in getting some, anymore, anyway." I lowered my voice. "I miss Faith."

"You what?" Trish emphatically turned off her treadmill and stepped aside. "You WHAT?!"

I turned off my treadmill and grabbed a towel. "I miss Faith."

"You've gotta be fucking kidding me, Marcella." Her jaw remained dropped. "You did everything for that girl. You finally cleaned up your act. You got off the drugs, you joined AA, you agreed to move to fucking California for crying out loud, AND you let her stay in your house out there after she dumps you." She shook her head. "You want her back? After all this, you want her back?"

"I do, yes." I smiled and shrugged. "Can't help it, Trish. The changes I made for her are the changes I've needed to make for a long time. She made me a better person, and I can't go back to who I was."

Trish rolled her eyes. "Oh, spare me the soliloquy. I'm not asking you to go back to being a drunken whore..."

"HEY!"

"I'm just saying, Macy, that she wasn't exactly appreciative of what you did for her."

I hung the towel around my neck. "Maybe she just needs some time."

"Maybe," she surrendered. "But still..."

"Maybe I'm still in love with her." I sighed. "I need her back in my life, Trish. I just wish I could have her back in my life."

"Be careful what you wish for." Trish snapped her towel at me. "Let's hit the sauna before we shower."

Chapter 43

"I'm so sorry about the crying." It was a normal reaction, I suppose, but I was still embarrassed. "It's just that shots..."

Renee smiled her nice, nursey smile. "Oh, it's nothing out of the ordinary. You two have a pleasant day."

Banky rubbed his arm and stared up at me, giggling. "Why are you crying, Mom? It didn't hurt."

"I am NOT crying," I sniffed, pulling down my shirtsleeve. "And if I was, it would be over all the little embryos who died so we could have flu shots."

"What?"

I often forgot I was talking to a five-year-old.

"Embryos, kid. They're in eggs. They make these shots out of eggs."

"Ohhhh." Now I'd made him nervous. "I don't like eggs."

"Well, this is one way to get them into you, even if you won't eat them."

Still nervous over the thought of someone injecting eggs into his system, Banky now spoke with less bravado. "Well, it didn't hurt."

"That's because you're a tough guy, Banks. You're a big, strong man, and I'm a mere fragile female." I lifted his arms. "Look at those muscles!" On cue, as we'd done this countless times, he growled and flexed his arms.

"Mom?" Thus began his hour long inquisition.

"Oui?"

"Why did we have to get flu shots?"

"So you won't throw up on me again at the checkout line in Valumart. That's why." I held out two lollipops the nurse had left for us.

"Red or purple?"

"Purple." I handed it to him, unwrapped. "Mom?"

I shifted my lollipop to answer him. "Yes?" I said, shifting my lollipop to speak.

"Why did you get a shot?"

"Because I'm old." I slipped the strap of my briefcase over my shoulder.

"How old?"

"As old as the dinosaurs, kid." I pulled his sweater over his head and fixed his hair with my fingers. "Come on, we've got places to go."

"Where are we going?" He followed me out into the waiting room, then down the hallway to the stairs.

"To look at a property we might buy."

"Another building?" he said, clapping.

Banky liked to explore prospective buildings and, due to his stature, agility, and overall eagerness to get dirty, he was a great set of eyes to bring along. The boy could sniff out a cockroach in broad daylight within seconds. He found leaks, cracks, and other tell-tale signs of impending expense with ease.

"Not a building, kid. A property." I crouched to let my eyes meet his. "A building or a space is something a person needs to start a business." I winked. "A property is what a businessperson wants to buy to RESELL to someone wanting to start a business."

"To make money."

"Yes." We continued on, descending the office stairs.

"Mom?"

"Yes, my inquisitive son covered in grape candy?"

"Is this your job?"

"No. I don't have a job." I stopped with unnecessary haste, checking my Palm Pilot to confirm the viewing appointment. "I'm retired."

And, having sold the travel agency, I was, really.

Sort of.

I guess.

"You're doing this to make money, but it's not a job?"

"I'm doing this because I'm not ready to be a dinosaur just yet." I checked my lipstick in a compact mirror and adjusted my cufflinks. "What do you think, is the bracelet too much with this suit?"

Banky cocked his head, curious. "It's the Jil Sander, right?"

I nodded.

He frowned. "Lose the bracelet."

What can I say? The kid knew his labels and accessories.

The office of Germaine, my old chum and doctor, had been dimly lit and smelled of alcohol swabs. Outside, however, the day was gorgeous.

Sunlight had managed to burn through the smog

early, and birds wove their songs throughout waves of traffic noise. I was just about to suggest we get ice cream after viewing the 48th Street prospect when my mobile rang.

"Hello? Hello?" Static. I hung up.

Banky spun around. "At the sound of a message, leave a tone...beep beep..." He was singing AND spinning now.

Banky, the perfect test subject for the yet to be released Ritalin dart gun.

"Oh, God...he's speaking in tongues!" I threw my hand to my forehead. "Sugar rush!"

He spun around two or three more times before wiping out on the grass.

"Come along, child." I thrust out my hand to help him to his feet. "This wind is COLD. You're putting on a hat as soon as we get to the car."

"Mom!" he whined.

"All right. I don't want to hear you bitching when you wake up with an earache, mister."

I turned away and heard him shuffling behind me, mumbling.

"Okay, okay, I'll wear a hat. Geez."

My phone rang, again.

"This is Macy Delongchamp," I answered it. Be a hardass and at least they'll give you the courtesy of apologizing for a wrong number. Sometimes, anyway.

I froze in my stride, not only to keep the signal, but because of what I heard.

"Miss Delongchamp, I have you listed as an emergency contact for Faith Littlefield."

The voice went on to tell of a motorcycle accident. Faith had been the passenger. They'd lost control and slammed into a guardrail.

She was in ICU. Critical. Pending surgery. Cracked pelvis, broken ribs. Something called a tension pneumothorax. And...

"Her *ear*!?" I lowered my voice, for Banky's sake. "Her *ear*?"

It was a lonely visual, an ear lying bodyless at the side of the road. It was a worse visual picturing Faith missing said ear. They'd found it, I guess, mostly intact, and it was to be reattached shortly, while the other elves in the workshop put pins in her broken pelvis and removed splinters of bone from the left side of her chest. She was stable, now, being prepped. Being 3,000 miles away, I'd never felt more impotent. I had to get there.

Lavinia happily agreed to let Banky crash with her and her son. Banky and John (named, obviously, for Lavinia's onetime Kennedy dream husband, a man she hoped we would all speculate as her son's secret father) had become close friends, and both seemed excited at the prospect of rooming together for a few days. I'd simply told Banky that his other mom had been in an accident, but would be fine, and I had to be there to sign some papers and be certain she was being taken care of properly. He accepted this explanation without question. Ah, the trust of a child. I was pleased that he felt I had the situation in hand and could continue playing and whistling without care. This was what being a good mother was about, allowing your child to feel safe on your watch of the world.

This is what I'd always felt in need of and had found at last with Vi, even with her flaws.

●

The motorcyclist in question had been sniffing around Faith since the party in Topanga. Faith had mentioned her with a flirtatious annoyance during our many phone conversations, saying, "A friend keeps bugging me to take a ride on her new bike." Britt, a slim blonde in a leather cycling suit, hair still flipped casually over one shoulder, sat up on a gurney with her leg in a soft cast. She'd obviously gotten the easier end of the deal.

"So you're the one responsible for this, huh?" I wasted no time in illustrating my intentions. "Well, listen here, Susie Quattro, she'd better come through all of this or so help me..."

She put up hand. "Uh...who the fuck are you?"

"I'm Faith Littlefield's wife," I said through clenched teeth. "That's who the fuck I am."

"Her *wha*...? Ohhhhh. Riiiiiight." She tapped her chin. "Her *ex*. The one who owns the house." She smiled. "Nice place."

"Goddamn you wannabe Jo from *Facts of Life*!" I lunged for her, managing to take hold of a fistful of hair and give it a good yank before a linebacker orderly pulled me back.

"Bring it, bitch!" Blonde Britt shook her fist. "You fight like a girl!"

"I *am* a girl!" I straightened my suit jacket, slipping my foot back into a heel I'd kicked astray in the ruckus. "You keep away from my wife, you understand?!"

A voice, calm and even, rose from behind me.

"Miss Delongchamp, I presume?"

A short, bespectacled dyke in a graying pageboy and green scrubs took me gently by the elbow. "Miss Littlefield's no longer in the ER, ma'am." She smiled. "I can take you to her room, if you like."

She was asleep when I got there, fresh from surgery and spent, blood still caked here and there at her hairline, bandages gracing half her head and the bridge of her nose. A tube jutted out from between two bruised ribs, her arms decorated with IVs. Faith looked as small and as helpless as I felt.

So this is how it feels, I thought. This is what it is to see everything you've ever loved thrashed to bits.

I paused, swallowing hard.

This is that special guilt reserved for such special occasions.

I rested my palms at the foot of the bed, staring up at her like a pastor from the pulpit.

"So here we are, again." Tears slipped through my smirk. "God, please..." I shut my eyes in concentration. "Faith." I went out on a limb. Would this hurt her or help? "I love you." I cleared my throat. "I love you, and I'm not going to let anything happen to you. I promise."

I couldn't help but recall not so long ago when our roles had been reversed: she at my bedside after my heart attack years before; me, stuck full of tubes, fading in and out, struggling to stay conscious so I might get one last look at my girl.

I winced at the memory.

She'd left me lying there.

I remembered, then, how it had felt to watch her walk away.

"How could you leave me like that?"

I shut my eyes hard, ashamed to be thinking this.

Even at my most selfless, I'm selfish.

"Fuck."

But I thought it anyway, and asked it, again: "How could you have left me there, dying, if you loved me?"

Faith remained unconscious, her chest rising and falling, the steady, strong rhythm of her heart rising in peaks on the green monitor screen.

"I told you not to go with that cycle dyke." I shook my head. "I told you, Faith. I told you she was no good."

I pulled a chair out from the wall and sat.

"I can't believe you fucked her."

Oh, Macy, stop being such a martyr. You're not the one who lost an ear.

I squeezed her foot beneath the covers.

"Such big feet for a little thing." I laughed past the lump in my throat, bowing my head. "My little, big-footed Indian girl."

Chapter 44

"Come on." I patted her arm with one hand, the peak-flow meter in the other. "Give it a try, huh? You broke your ribs. You gotta do this, kid, or you'll end up back in that hospital room with those awful drapes."

Faith frowned. "It's going to hurt like hell, Macy. You know when doctors tell you 'You may experience some discomfort,' it's going to hurt like crazy."

She had a point.

"It might, initially, but…" I sighed. "Oh, hell. I'll go first. Always wanted to know what it was like to give a blowjob, anyway."

I took the tiny hose in hand and huffed into it. The ball rose half way up the tube. I held it there for a few seconds, then explosively choked. Faith laughed.

"Well, I know I can do better than THAT."

Thus began her long recovery from the accident.

Pork chops. Mashed potatoes. Green beans. Garnish, even.

Dang.

Trish came to California to stay with us for a bit to help out. The balanced meal before me was one of many benefits of having her around. I tended to Faith and shuttled her to physical therapy. Trish helped with Banky and the house.

"What's with you?" Trish slid a plate before me and sat down. "You're all smiles, today. What gives?"

I blushed. "She kissed me."

"Well, it's about time! You've been her slave for a month!" Trish paused. "Lips or cheek?"

"Lips." I giggled. "Softly. Gently." I giggled, again. "Sweetly."

"Oh, brother." Trish rolled her eyes. "So, you think you two will get back together, officially?"

I smiled so broadly my face hurt. "I think so."

"I KNOW so!" Banky marched up to the table. "What's for dinner?"

"Pork chops." I swung him up onto my lap. "And how do you know this, oh, wise one?"

"I asked God," he said, matter-of-factly, sticking a finger into my mashed potatoes. "I saw you wiping Mom's butt last week, and I thought, *"Boy, she really loves her! I wouldn't wipe anybody's butt!"* So I asked God to make you be married again."

"There you have it," Trish said. "Let the reunion commence."

For six weeks, Faith was unable to bear weight on one side. A walker, and occasionally my less-than-brawny arms, helped her scuttle about the house, but to rebuild the muscle in her legs, she worked with a physical therapist three times a week. Our pool was undergoing a desperately needed renovation, but there was a pool at the rec center up the street, and we often met there for mobility exercises in the water.

On this day, however, this overcast afternoon in the canyon, all lights were out when we passed through the double doors. I locked them behind us.

"Well, now…" I stepped out of my heels and began unbuttoning my blouse. "Are you ready for your mobility exercises?"

"Macy! What…?" She laughed. "What are you doing?"

"Stripping." I flung my skirt over my shoulder. It hit the wall. "Come on. You're next. You do your top half, I'll help with the bottom."

"What?!"

"Go on. Don't be such a prude," I said, now nakedly at the helm of her wheelchair, backing us through another set of doors and into a dark room illuminated only by floating candles. "It's just us."

"We're alone? But…" She smiled. "You can't rent out a public pool."

"Honey, you can rent Cleveland for the right money." I moved to the pool's edge and pulled a bottle from a bucket of ice. "Non-alcoholic, which is lame, I know, but…"

"I don't think it's lame at all." She pulled off her shirt. "And this is much better than Cleveland."

"I'm glad you feel that way, though Cleveland may have been easier to book." I handed her a flute of the benign beverage, fumbling for the portable stereo. "Here we are." The music began.

"Nice." She took a sip and smiled. "Roberta Flack."

"Of course. I'd originally selected Devo, but I didn't think you'd be up for it." I extended my hand. "Care to dance?"

"Macy, I..." She sighed. "I can't."

"Of course you can. I cleared it with Hitler." I leaned over. "Put your arms around my neck. There. There we are." I raised up. "Now hold on."

And there we were, suddenly flat against each other, naked. Faith balanced precariously on her toes. I tensed my shoulders to give her at least the impression of un-yielding support. I had an urge, then, looking into her eyes and feeling our bodies moving together for the first time in forever. I had the urge to lift her legs and wrap them around my waist, rubbing our perfectly trimmed selves together until we fell to the floor and explored what desperately needed to be explored in each other. But, alas, she was still on the mend, and, alas, my back was killing me. I opted for the sensible risk of taking baby steps down into the pool.

The buoyancy helped us loosen our grips and relax a bit. I rested my hands at the small of her back and guided her carefully.

"The first tiiiime....ever I sawwww your faaaace..."

Faith laughed. "You're a terrible singer."

"And you're a lousy dancer. Stop being such a butch and follow my lead."

"I know what all this is for." She smiled. "In case you were wondering."

I nodded. "Our anniversary."

"I can't believe you remembered it."

I pressed my cheek to hers. "How could I forget

finding you mugged at my stoop? You're lucky it was only a mild concussion."

"I was lucky to be rescued." She pressed her lips to my ear. "You were so gentle, so gallant."

"I was mad for you." My voice quivered. "Completely mad."

Faith pulled back and looked up at me. "Macy, I've never felt what I feel for you with anyone. Ever."

The music ended. I pulled her to me. I kissed her.

"So," I shifted my feet rhythmically. "Where were we?"

"Duh." She laughed. "There's no music."

"Don't let that stop us."

Faith lay her head against my chest. "So, where do you think we're going with this, this time?"

I stroked her hair. "Well, I know I'm not going anywhere."

Epilogue

Twelve years have passed.

We're seated in a noisy high school gymnasium, a group of boys clustered at one side of an enormous burgundy mat. Two struggle and grapple for a stronghold in the center. My interest in them is only peripheral; I focus on our boy.

This boy is tall and slender, a body more suited for basketball or swimming, rising far above his stocky teammates. He seems older than most of them, but isn't. He slips out of the straps of his wrestling singlet nonchalantly, slowly revealing a torso taught with muscle. I chuckle because I know he is very much aware of his body and the attention it must be getting from some of the women, some of the men and boys, most of the girls.

This boy has little interest in college, seeing it only as a means to an end to achieving the foundation for his career. He is the only boy his age to work summers without pay at a real estate agency. He plans to eventually coax investors into refurbishing high-rise office and apartment buildings in Manhattan, selling or leasing them for enormous profit. He's been focused on this rather lofty goal for years.

Back in the stands, I smile, content that life has continued nicely. Faith busies herself with a number of charitable causes. She plays tennis and I occasionally join her, enjoying smog-free lungs and a now smoothly running heart with a two-year-old synthetic mitral valve. She and I travel abroad. We take ballroom dancing lessons at the rec center. The sex is about once a week, and it's actually pretty good.

The boy still stands slightly apart from his peers, observing quietly as the others frantically cheer. I center him in my thoughts. He is vain. He is charming. He doesn't always make the best decisions. He is secretly quite compassionate.

A girl of high school age with college curves walks past him. He lets his eyes drift to her. I catch his gaze. We smile at each other.

This boy knows a fantastic ass when he sees one.

Just like his mother.